'Creates a gloriously Gothic atmosphere of suspense' Amanda Craig, *The Times*

'All the ingredients of an enthralling adventure – a lonely child, a missing parent, a series of clues and a surprisingly satisfying twist of an ending' *Daily Mail*

'Shot through with mystery, this is a deliciously old-fashioned story . . . A touching journey of discovery filled with atmosphere and surprise' Julia Eccleshare, *Guardian*

'Despite its cold and stark setting, *The Haunting of Charity Delafield* is a heart-warming tale of friendship, family and love with an uplifting, magical twist' *Booktrust*

'An elegant, atmospheric tale, with frost and mystery and a bit of magic' *Independent on Sunday*

'A deliciously eerie tale' *Daily Telegraph*

The Haunting of Charity Delafield

IAN BECK

CORGI

THE HAUNTING OF CHARITY DELAFIELD
A CORGI BOOK 978 0 552 56206 5

First published in Great Britain by The Bodley Head,
an imprint of Random House Children's Publishers UK
A Random House Group Company

The Bodley Head edition published 2011
This edition published 2012

1 3 5 7 9 10 8 6 4 2

Text and illustrations copyright © Ian Beck, 2011

The Random House Group Limited supports the Forest Stewardship Council (FSC®),
the leading international forest certification organization. Our books carrying the FSC
label are printed on FSC®-certified paper. FSC is the only forest certification scheme
endorsed by the leading environmental organizations, including Greenpeace. Our paper
procurement policy can be found at www.randomhouse.co.uk/environment.

MIX
Paper from
responsible sources
FSC® C016897

Set in Baskerville MT 13/18

RANDOM HOUSE CHILDREN'S PUBLISHERS UK
61–63 Uxbridge Road, London W5 5SA

www.**randomhousechildrens**.co.uk
www.**totallyrandombooks**.co.uk
www.**randomhouse**.co.uk

Addresses for companies within The Random House Group Limited can be found at:
www.randomhouse.co.uk/offices.htm

THE RANDOM HOUSE GROUP Limited Reg. No. 954009

A CIP catalogue record for this book is available from the British Library.

Printed and bound in Great Britain by CPI Group (UK), Croydon, CR0 4YY

For Daisy and Laurence Howarth

From the *County Mercury*
December 16th 1903

COUNTY MERCURY

LOCAL MYSTERY STILL UNSOLVED; POLICE CLOSE THE CASE

Twelve years ago, almost to the day, Mrs Ariella Delafield, wife of prominent local landowner Mr Charles Delafield of Stone Green Hall, disappeared without a trace. Despite the best efforts of the local police force, household staff, friends and family, no explanation of how or why she disappeared has ever been found; nor has there been any sign of her in the intervening years, in spite of extensive searches of the house, the garden and the local forest.

Mrs Delafield has never since contacted her husband, or her young daughter, Miss Charity Delafield, who was only six months old at the time of her mother's disappearance. Mr Delafield has retreated from public life since the tragic occurrence, keeping his young daughter under strict and safe supervision. The mysterious case, which has baffled the police and the public for these last twelve years, was finally declared closed today by local police chief Commander Bartholomew.

Mr Delafield was unavailable for comment.

Chapter One

The corridor stretched out in front of Charity. It seemed to be getting longer, and the door at the end seemed to get further away as she walked through the flickering darkness. She held the candle in its holder very carefully. She was mindful that it might start a fire, and that would not please her father. The windows along the corridor appeared to be open – not very wide, but enough to let in the night wind, which stirred the long white curtains so that they blew inwards like sails as she walked past. She shielded the candle with her hand. It would only need one edge of the fine muslin and lace to catch on the naked flame . . .

Shadows flickered and moved all around her. She caught the movements out of the corner of her eye. Looming shapes curled darkly up the walls and flitted across the ceiling – partly Charity's own shadow as it moved along the corridor, and partly the shadows of the shrouded marble busts and statues that lined the way. There was a gentle slope upwards, a gradual tilt to the floor, and the further she walked, the more effort it took, as if she were suddenly climbing a steep hill. The ceiling seemed to be getting lower too. If she went much further, she would have to crouch down.

Charity saw Mr Tompkins ahead of her – a black shape in the shadowed darkness. 'Where are you going?' she shouted to him.

'You know,' he called back. 'Come on, nearly there.'

She dropped the candle and heard it roll

across the floor. The flame went out at once. All she could see was the tiny red dot of failing heat at the end of the wick. She could smell the spatters of hot wax too, and the drifting curls of candle smoke, which seemed to be spelling something out, making letters in the air. She was left bending over under the low ceiling in complete darkness, trying to read them.

Suddenly she felt the tap of something warm on her face.

'Now,' she said out loud, her eyes shut tight.

'Now,' she said into the cold emptiness of her bedroom.

Mr Tompkins was there, sitting on her pillow. He patted Charity's face a second time with his soft, midnight-black paw, and then she sat up in bed.

It had been the dream again.

It was always the same dream – when she remembered it, that is. Sometimes she did remember it after she woke up, but during the dream itself, while it was actually happening, she never realized that she had had it before. It seemed new and freshly minted every time. The long walk along the dark corridor was always accompanied by a feeling of anticipation, the expectation of a secret delight to come.

Charity sometimes asked herself why she had never told Rose or anyone else in the house about the recurring dream. She knew the answer instinctively, although she couldn't explain it. She was sure that she dreamed it over and over again for a reason, and that the reason was hers alone. She simply knew that she just shouldn't mention it to anyone. It was her own little bit of secret knowledge, and one day she was sure she would come to understand it.

It was morning now, and she sighed to herself and stretched her arms up.

'Hello old pusscat, Mr Tompkins,' she said, and ruffled his ears. The cat rubbed against her and purred. 'If Rose finds you in here she'll put you out, and I'll be in trouble again,' she added, lifting him down onto the floor. He looked up at her with his mysterious green eyes. She could always talk to Mr Tompkins, and he understood everything she said. At least, he seemed to.

'Shoo,' she said, and clapped her hands lightly, but Mr Tompkins just sat and looked up at her, opened his mouth and gave a silent *Meow*.

'In a minute, then,' she told him.

She knew that at any moment, as regular as clockwork, Rose would come in and light the fire, as she did every morning, and another day would start, just like all the others.

Chapter Two

Charity lived in a big dark house called Stone Green Hall. It had sharp pointed gables and tall windows and high, wide chimneys. It stood all on its own, shadowing the rise of the hill. It had two wings projecting out on either side, to the west and to the east. The old house was surrounded by a starkly formal garden, which was the size of a park. High, closely spaced iron railings surrounded the house and garden. Beyond them was a road, and beyond the road was the tangle of dark trees that made up an ancient forest.

The house had miles of long corridors, some

of which looked like the insides of old sailing ships with their curved and darkly varnished wooden ceilings. Many of the rooms down these corridors were locked. Their dark doors were the colour of the conkers that Charity might find in the park around the house in the autumn. They stood to attention, mute, one after the other. They were off limits and forbidden to everyone, including Charity. They had been like that for as long as anyone could remember.

'You don't need to go into those rooms, and that is my last word on the subject,' her father had said when she had first asked about them.

There were deep, dark corners and shrouded shapes all over the house. There were pictures on walls, marble busts on columns and full-length statues, and they were all covered up with white dustsheets. They were often piled together in the darkest areas, so that at bedtime they seemed to lurk together in packs, as if specially designed to frighten her. She couldn't understand why they were treated like that, neglected, as if they were unwanted.

There were trophies too: all sorts of dusty, sad animal heads mounted on boards – deer with their fine proud antlers, badgers' masks, and rows of fox heads, with landscapes and suggestions of skies painted behind them. They were spread all along the corridors in glass-fronted boxes, and there were even some in the main drawing room too. It would seem that the house had once belonged to a hunter. Charity's father did not hunt now, as far as she knew, although he was often away on something called 'business' – whatever that meant.

The main rooms downstairs were kept to a high standard by the small number of staff, but in other places, like the high attics, or the long corridor that led to the bathroom on the nursery floor, not much was done in the way of maintenance.

Charity got out of bed. She shivered and

pulled back the curtains. A surprise waited for her: the inside of the window was partly frosted over, and outside, snowflakes were falling. Snow was an event, and Charity's quiet and strictly ordered life had almost no events in it at all. She rubbed the traces of frost away from the glass and then picked up Mr Tompkins.

'Look,' she said. 'It's snowing.'

Mr Tompkins gave a soft *Meow*.

The snow fell slowly, and the flakes twisted around one another in the air as they fell, so that they almost seemed to be dancing together. 'The snow is settling, covering everything,' Charity whispered in the cat's ear. It was true. From her high window she watched it fall, gently transforming the ordinary. She watched the snow cover her day-to-day world with white, flake by flake, like a slow magic trick.

It reminded her of something from when she was much younger – from a time long ago, before she thought she could remember anything.

She put Mr Tompkins down, went over to the cupboard and rummaged about for a moment. There at the back, among her piled-up boots and shoes, was an old spinning top, with clear panels of thick glass on the sides. She took it out and balanced it on the floor. She pressed the little plunger up and down a few times, and then she let the top spin. As it spun it made a sweet sound, a suspended chord of music, and tiny snowflakes spun and fell behind the glass; and there, as if somehow in the distance, a tiny white unicorn reared up and down with the movement of the top. Watching and listening to it made her feel odd and dreamy and very small again.

Mr Tompkins reached out a paw to the spinning top, but Charity gently took it away again. 'Let it play,' she said. 'Let it gallop.' As she stroked Mr Tompkins's head she watched the little dancing snowflakes float past the unicorn while the top spun, and the music almost seemed to slow down time itself.

All at once Charity remembered that there was another event to look forward to. She had been given eight small squares of forbidden chocolate. They had been smuggled to her by Edward, the young footman. He had hidden them for Charity inside the saddle bag of her old rocking horse. She was excited about unwrapping the gold foil – somehow, some-where – and eating the sweet squares.

It was then that Rose came in, carrying a bucket of fresh coals. 'Good morning,' she said brightly. 'Up already?'

'It's snowing,' Charity said excitedly, turning from the window with the rarest of things across her pale face: a broad smile.

'Miss Manners is not up yet, then, I see . . .' Rose said drily.

'Sorry, Rose,' said Charity, and she gave a little curtsey. 'Good morning. But look – it really is snowing.'

'You don't have to tell me,' Rose said. 'Who do

you think had to walk through it to break the ice on the bird bath first thing this morning, before breakfast?' She shook her head, then saw Mr Tompkins. 'Out you go now, you awful old mog.' She held the door open, and Mr Tompkins slipped silently out.

Rose looked down at the spinning top. 'Whatever made you get that old toy out, Miss Charity?' she asked. 'As far as I remember you'll be thirteen next birthday, not three.'

'I know,' said Charity. 'I was remembering the sound it made and the little scene inside, that was all. The snow made me think of it.'

'Well, I wonder if you might put it away now, please,' Rose said, 'because knowing my luck I'll trip over it.'

Rose lit the fire and, once Charity was dressed, persuaded her to sit down in front of the looking glass. She smiled briskly at Charity's reflection, but Charity did not smile back at her.

It was time for Rose to brush Charity's hair.

Charity's hair was fine and easily tangled, and depending on the light, sometimes it was the colour of bright gold, and sometimes it was the colour of flames.

'Hold still, now, and it won't hurt you,' said Rose, as she always did. But it hurt, whether you held still, or wriggled, and writhed, and screamed, and kicked your feet against the skirting board under the dressing table, as Charity used to.

Charity frowned at herself and Rose in the silver-edged glass.

It hurt.

Charity's hair was curly and knotted, and the brush pulled hard in swift, deadly strokes down her head with a static crackle.

'Ow!' murmured the girl, who would not cry now – who would certainly not let Rose see her cry again. 'Ow!'

'There, all done, and such a fuss,' said Rose, who had been counting carefully as she brushed.

'Seventy-five strokes, morning and night. That's the rule – that's the way Mr Delafield likes it.' She nodded, as if to remind herself of the strict routine.

She carefully picked all Charity's loose hairs free from the brush. She rolled the fine golden strands into a ball and put them straight into the fire, watching as the sparks of burning hair twisted and leaped up the dark chimney. Then Rose put down the brush with a satisfied nod. She spun Charity round by the shoulders, away from the looking glass, and said, 'Time for something special this morning: first, breakfast with your father, and then we are to take a walk.'

'Breakfast with Father?' said Charity. 'Oh.' Her face fell a little and her eyes betrayed her worry at the thought.

'He asked especially to see you this morning,' Rose said, patting her on the arm. 'Then we'll have a nice walk out in the snow,' she added.

'Yes, a walk.' Charity turned back to the window

and the dancing snow. Her eyes widened and the smile returned to her lips. 'Outside in the snow.'

'Yes, it's that time again. Time for a walk outside,' said Rose, pleased to have sprung a surprise – or at least a change to Charity's strict routine. 'I'll fetch your outdoor coat from the wardrobe.'

Charity quickly took the squares of chocolate out of the saddle bag on her old rocking horse and tucked them into her pinafore-dress pocket. She loved her old rocking horse. If Rose hadn't been coming back so soon, she would have climbed on and rocked dreamily for a while. She set it going with her hand anyway.

Rose returned with Charity's bright red wool coat with its rows of black buttons, and her black hat and muff. Charity could feel the happy weight of the squares of chocolate in their foil wrapping while she stood at the window, watching the long avenue and the falling, skipping, dancing flakes of snow.

Chapter Three

Rose and Charity left the nursery and set off along one of the long, gloomy corridors. There was no sign of Charity's father, which was not unusual. Mr Tompkins trotted along behind them, keeping to the shadows.

As usual, the lower floors of the house were ordered and calm, with the quiet sounds of ticking clocks and crackling fires. In the main entrance hallway there was a fireplace so tall that you could stand up inside it. When they reached it, they heard the ringing scrape of a shovel from somewhere outside the front door. Rose said,

'That'll be Edward, clearing the snow from the paths.' She knocked on the door of the study.

'Come,' a voice called out, and Rose opened the door.

Mr Delafield was already at the table and halfway through his breakfast. He had some documents spread out in front of him. He stood up when Rose and Charity came in, dabbing at his mouth with a white napkin. 'Good morning, Rose, and good morning, my dear,' he said. 'Charity, do come and sit opposite me here at the table. It has been a while since we have seen one another.'

'Good morning, Father,' Charity said, and made a deep curtsey, hoping the forbidden chocolate would not show in her pocket.

Rose fetched a bowl of porridge for her.

'Thank you,' Charity said carefully and politely.

Across the table her father looked searchingly at her with his usual mournful expression. 'Your hair is looking especially fine this morning, Charity. Very neatly done, Rose. It is not easy to keep it looking like that, I know.'

'Thank you, sir,' Rose replied.

'Will you have some breakfast with us, Rose?' He gestured at the sideboard. 'There are Loch Fyne kippers – excellent brain food – and there is porridge or fresh kedgeree.'

'No, thank you, sir,' Rose said. 'I ate my breakfast earlier with Mrs Browne in the kitchen.'

'Good, good,' he said distractedly. 'In that case, I wonder, Rose, if you might leave us alone for a moment?'

Rose went out and closed the darkly varnished door after her.

'Is the porridge to your liking?' Mr Delafield asked his daughter.

'Yes, thank you, Father,' she said.

'Good. We have not spoken for a few weeks now, and I have some news that I want to share with you.'

'News, Father?' All sorts of thoughts and images suddenly tumbled into Charity's head – and none of them good.

'Yes, news. It is to do with your education. I know that Rose is an excellent and intelligent person, and that you are very fond of her, and that she schools you in the basic subjects as best she can. She plays her part as your governess and tutor admirably, but only up to a point.'

Charity felt herself trembling. She feared what was coming next. She didn't want her father to see her spoon suddenly shaking over her thick, barely sweetened porridge, so she rested her wrist firmly against the edge of the table.

'In June you will reach your thirteenth birthday. Thirteen . . .' he said, almost to himself. 'I can hardly believe it. The time has gone so fast . . .'

Charity noticed that the colour had drained from his face and his hands were gripping the table. 'Are you all right, Father?' she asked. 'Are you ill?'

He sat silently for a moment, staring beyond her, as if something frightening had just come into the room. Then he blinked and came back to the present. 'You are rapidly becoming a young lady. You will soon have outgrown the simplicities of governess-led tuition, and to that end I have found a suitable establishment which is willing to take you.'

'An establishment? What is that, Father?'

'A school, in effect – albeit a special school, run on clear, rational and scientific lines. A school specializing in educating and helping girls just like yourself.'

'A school?' Charity echoed, looking up at her father.

'Yes, a school. You are not a parrot, my dear. There really is no need to repeat everything I say.'

'Sorry, Father . . . Where is the school?' Charity spoke quietly, but with a sense of dread. She hoped that the school would be somewhere close to the house, but feared the worst.

'It is in Norfolk, close to a town called Cromer, and so it is near the sea.'

'Is that far away, Father?'

'I should say a hundred miles or so from here, give or take a mile or two.'

A hundred miles seemed impossibly far away. Charity gaped at her father.

'It is a boarding institution, Charity. You will, of course, stay there during term time.'

'I'll come back for the holidays, though, Father, won't I?' Charity said, a rising panic taking hold of her so that she screwed up her napkin in her hands.

'I am not sure . . .' Her father hesitated, aware of the anguish in his daughter's face. 'The holiday periods will enable you to take supervised expeditions to the seaside and so forth. I believe it will be very enjoyable for you. Here – look for yourself.'

He pushed a printed brochure across the table. The front cover showed a building very like an old castle, complete with battlements. It was even darker-looking than Stone Green Hall. *Lowering Castle*, she read. *Institute of Rational and Scientific Education.* This was printed across the top of the brochure in heavy black Gothic lettering.

'There will be other girls of your own age there. I am conscious that I have neglected you in the area of such friendships, but with your condition . . .' Mr Delafield let the word hang in the air between them.

'Yes, Father.' Charity quickly looked down at the brochure so as not to catch his eye. She was only too aware of what a disappointment she was to him. Her poor mother had died giving birth to her, and then, of course, there was the question of her 'condition' – a word always uttered in hushed tones, but entirely unexplained. She had no idea what it really meant, and even though she had asked, she had never been able to find out what her condition actually was. From an early age she had simply been told, again and again,

24

that she had a condition which made her different from everybody else in some way; which needed special treatment.

She was not allowed to run, or to explore much of her own house, or to leave the grounds. In fact, she was not allowed outside at all, except under strict supervision. She was discouraged from reading books of fairy tales and mythology – indeed, her father had gradually taken them all from her library, replacing them with books on science and mathematics. No one ever visited the house except tradespeople, for deliveries and so forth. She never saw so much as a local newspaper. She had no friends except for the kindly staff in the house, and Mr Tompkins. She had never even met another child of her own age. She was kept as a pampered prisoner.

Charity's father spoke again. 'If you have finished your porridge, you may take the bowl over to the sideboard and then rejoin Rose. I have allowed a walk around the whole park for your exercise today. It is not every day that we have such a thing as a fall of snow.'

'Thank you, Father. I do like the snow,' Charity said, biting her lower lip and doing her best not to cry at the prospect of being sent away from Rose and Edward and Mrs Browne – and, of course, Mr Tompkins, who had once been her mother's kitten and was now Charity's cat. She loved Mr Tompkins very much, and the thought of not seeing him was impossible to take in.

She stood up and folded her napkin carefully, tucking it back into her monogrammed ivory napkin ring. She took her bowl to the sideboard. While her back was turned to him, her father said, 'You will join your new school in May, before your birthday. Of course, the new school year will not begin until September, but I gather many of the students live there throughout the summer, and this will give you plenty of opportunity to get to know your classmates before your lessons begin. It is possible that we might visit the institution prior to that. It will be something of an outing for us, perhaps.'

'Yes, Father,' Charity said, turning and dropping a respectful curtsey, and feeling the friendly weight of the forbidden chocolate in her pocket.

There was a sudden howling noise from somewhere high up on the roof. A freak gust of wind curled itself around the gables, blowing the settled snow off in white gusts, and then hurled itself down the big chimneys.

The wind scattered soot and snow and grey smoke out of the fireplace into the breakfast room in a great dark cloud. Charity stepped back, covering her face, and her father jumped up as the acrid smoke curled itself over him like a threatening shadow.

'Tell Rose to send for Edward. We will need the town chimney sweep here as soon as possible,' he said, coughing and covering his mouth with his napkin.

Chapter Four

'Stand nice and still now.'

Rose helped Charity into her long red winter coat with its double row of twenty black buttons down the front. Charity looked up at her. She wanted to say something about being sent away, but knew she would burst into tears if she did, so she said nothing.

Rose smoothed down the front of the coat, then spun Charity round and smoothed down the back, with its buttoned half-belt, until she was a neat red parcel. She handed Charity her muff to keep her hands warm, and put the Russian-style hat on her head. Charity avoided Rose's gaze and looked back down the corridor, where Mr Tompkins sat washing his paws.

Rose opened the back door. Outside, the wind was still rattling against the rooftops, and layers of powdery snow blew over them like clouds. They stepped out into the shock of the cold air. The heavy snow clouds were billowing away over the forest, and the sky above the garden was now patched with fragments of clear, icy blue. All around the grounds stood narrow black lines of the high iron railings, their pointed tops as sharp as arrowheads and as deadly as knife blades. There were lines of stone statues, too – all wrapped up for the winter with coarse sacking, and tied up with string. Their shadows were blue where they lay across the fresh fall of snow.

Rose and Charity marched down the middle of the avenue between the lines of tall, clipped square trees and sacking-covered statues, like a prisoner and her escort. Mr Tompkins trotted along behind them, lifting his paws carefully up out of the snow with every step.

Sure enough, Edward was out clearing the snow, and he stood up straight as they approached. He leaned on the handle of his shovel, and as they passed he nodded and called out a friendly, 'Good morning, Miss Charity! Good morning, Miss Rose!' He even nodded politely to Mr Tompkins.

Rose said, 'Mr Delafield needs you to send for the chimney sweep from town, Edward.'

He rested the spade against the wide base of a covered statue. 'Job's never done here, eh, Miss Rose?' he said cheerfully, and went back into the house, winking at Charity as he passed.

Charity felt some relief, at least, in being out of the house and in the fresh air. She walked behind Rose, her hands tucked into her muff, and thought about being sent away in just a few short months to that gloomy-looking castle. A tear slid down her cold cheek.

She felt angry as well as sad. She wished she could kick her tightly buttoned black boots into the snow drifts. She wished she could make a snowball and throw it at Rose, and knock her hat off her head. She wished Rose could throw a snowball back at her, then chase her round and round the garden, away from the avenue of sharply cut best-behaviour trees, in and out of the statues, and the clipped box hedges. She wished, just once, for something wild – for Rose to laugh, and tickle her, or call her a silly goose.

But she knew that none of this would ever happen; not in her strictly controlled world – and not with her condition.

At the end of the long avenue stood a pair of tall black iron gates, which were chained shut and firmly padlocked. When Charity and Rose had reached the gates, they would turn left, east-wards, and walk all the way round the huge garden, past the east wing of the big house, and then along the back. Then they would go round the west wing, which was locked up and neglected, and covered in twisted old climbing roses with thick trunks, and a dense growth of ivy. Then, once they were back at the front of the house, they would walk back up the avenue between the straight line of trees. They always did.

The air was so cold that when Charity breathed out her breath misted white. But even with the cold she feared that her secret chocolate, the one thing cheering her up, would soon melt in her pocket. She knew she would have to distract Rose, and then she might be able to eat it.

'Brrr!' she said suddenly. She came to a halt and stood shivering on the spot. 'It's so cold.' She stamped her boots up and down.

'Are you all right?' Rose said, turning. She saw that tears had tracked down Charity's face. 'Whatever is the matter?'

'I'm just cold. Rose, I need my scarf.'

'Oh, now, that was very silly of me,' Rose said,

and then hesitated. On no account was Charity to be left alone. This was always the first and strictest order given by Mr Delafield. She looked across the road beyond the gates and then into the wild dark trees beyond. Then she looked up and down the empty winding road. Nothing.

'I'll just ask Edward to keep an eye on you, and then I'll go and fetch your scarf,' she told Charity with a reluctant sigh. 'Edward?' she called out. 'Could you come over here a moment, do you think?'

'Hold on, then, miss,' Edward said. With his back turned to them, he took up his shovel and quickly obliterated the word *Rose*, surrounded by a heart, that he had drawn in the snow. He was delighted to have an excuse to talk to Rose. He came over, shouldering his spade like a soldier carrying a rifle.

'I have to go and fetch Miss Charity a warm scarf,' Rose said.

'I'm meant to go into town shortly, miss –

to fetch the chimney sweep,' Edward explained.

'It's only for a moment, Edward.' Rose smiled sweetly at him.

'Right you are, then. I'll wait here with her till you get back,' he said. 'Plenty to do this morning.' He turned away and continued shovelling snow from the path.

Rose told Charity, 'Now stay here, right here.' She pointed down at her feet. 'Stay on this very spot, and not a step further, mind.' She turned and hurried back up the avenue to the house.

'Cold enough for you, miss?' Edward said with his back to her, bent low over his spade.

'Oh yes – brrr,' said Charity, walking very slowly backwards away from him, trying her best not to get tangled up with Mr Tompkins, who was snaking around her legs. Finally she was at the tall iron gates, which was the nearest she had ever been to the outside world. It was as if there was an invisible something, like a spell or a hex, that kept her inside.

Mr Tompkins had curled his tail around her ankles and stood, poised, looking out through the railings. He could easily have squeezed through and run off into the forest to go hunting, but he didn't, and as far as Charity knew he never had. She bent down and patted him while he stared up at her.

Charity leaned back against the gate, facing the house. She quickly pulled the squares of chocolate in their bright gold foil from her pocket. Eight sweet, dark squares. She opened her mouth, ready.

Then the cat suddenly stepped back towards the house, and an unexpected voice spoke quietly from behind Charity.

'You're just like her, my dear.'

Chapter Five

Charity turned round. An old woman stood there, a bright smile on her weathered face; she had appeared as if from nowhere. She wore ragged clothes and was bent over, with a big bundle of kindling across her back, held in place with a tattered shawl. Charity felt a strange shiver go through her, which was nothing to do with the cold. It was more a sense of recognition – something about what the old lady had said. Her skin prickled, and the hair on the back of her neck stood up.

The woman hobbled closer to the gate and lowered her bundle of sticks and mossy logs to the ground. Charity could see the ropes of blue veins spread across the back of her pale, cold-looking hands, and her eyes, which were the grey-green of murky river water.

She spoke again: 'I am so pleased to have found you at last. I have passed by here on many a cold morning, always hoping to catch you, my dear. You are your mother's daughter all right. I suppose he keeps you shut away in the big house, and the servants make you fires, with good dry coals, and bring you meals? I must fetch my own kindling, and build my own fire, and tend to my own pot.' She smiled kindly at Charity. 'Anyway, the time is coming . . .' She shifted the big bundle with her foot and sighed.

'Your mother was a rare beauty,' she added, 'and her hair was just like yours, the same colour exactly – like midsummer sunlight shining on cloth of gold.'

'You knew my mother?' Charity said, astonished.

'Why, bless you, my girl, of course I did! I was the midwife who helped you come into the world. I saw you when you were a little mewling first-born, and but a minute old.'

Charity stared at the old lady on the other side of the iron railings in disbelief. She just had to find out more.

'Were you there when she . . . when my mother . . . died?' she asked very quietly, feeling tears welling up again.

The woman shook her head. 'Is that what they told you? That she died?'

'Yes,' Charity said.

The old lady shook her head mysteriously.

'Isn't that true?' Charity said.

The old lady shook her head again.

Charity could not believe it. She had been told that her poor mother had died in childbirth, and here was an old woman who knew differently. Was it all a lie? she wondered. Desperate to know more, she felt a strange emotion welling up inside her – a kind of hope that the story she had always been given was not true. She could feel herself trembling, and it was not because of the cold. Apart from her father, this was the first person whom she had ever spoken to, as far as she knew, who had actually known her mother. She had to keep her there somehow.

'Are you hungry?' Charity asked.

'Always hungry, my dear girl,' the old lady replied.

Charity pushed the gold-wrapped squares of chocolate out through the narrow bars of the gate.

The woman stared at them in disbelief. 'Why, bless you – gold . . .' she said, her eyes widening, and she reached out and took the bright squares from Charity.

'No, sorry,' Charity whispered. 'It's not gold, it's just chocolate.'

'Bless you, bless you. You have handed me a gift; you are a good child, you are a good, kind child. You are as good and kind and lovely as your mother, and I need to tell you something important.'

'What is it?' Charity said eagerly.

'A simple message,' the old lady told her. 'Just this: *Find the horn before your thirteenth birthday*.'

'Is that it?' Charity asked. 'What does it mean? It makes no sense.'

'Just carry on looking, keep your wits about you, and you will know what it means,' the woman said with a broad smile. Then she bent down again, put out her hand and tickled Mr Tompkins's ears. 'You're here too, then?' she said. 'I remember him as a little kitten. Cute as a button, he was.' She winked at Charity, then wearily hoisted the bundle of kindling onto her back again.

Edward suddenly straightened up from clearing the path. He turned and saw Charity, right over by the gate, talking to the old woman. 'Oh dear,' he said to himself, and set off towards them.

The clack of Rose's boots on the cleared part of the avenue echoed behind them suddenly.

'Oh no!' she shouted. 'Now, you just come away from that gate – and as quick as you like, miss!'

Mr Tompkins ran back up the path, but Charity stayed where she was. The old woman, with a sudden scowl and a look of defiance in her pale eyes, moved quickly away from the gate. The gold wrapping on the chocolate shone for an instant like a sunburst against her tattered grey shawl. She quickly hid the bright squares, tucking them away under the fringe.

'I don't understand it at all,' Charity said quietly to her. 'Shall I see you again?'

But Rose sent the old woman on her way with a flick of her hand.

Edward tapped on the railings with the flat blade of his spade and called out, 'Best stay away now,' after her. He dropped the shovel onto the path with a clang. A whole flock of rooks rose up from the trees, cawing and squawking.

'What on earth was going on, Edward?' Rose said. 'You were a bit slow on the uptake.'

'Sorry – got carried away with the shovelling. Feeling a bit dreamy today,' Edward said.

'Imagine what he would have said if he had seen that,' Rose sighed.

The old woman was already disappearing up the road, bent under the weight of the damp wooden bundle. She turned her head to look back, and nodded and smiled at Charity.

'I know, I know, I'm sorry,' Edward said, looking at Rose from under his fringe of tousled dark hair with a pleading look in his eyes. 'I'd better go, anyway – off to the sweep's . . .' He hesitated, not wanting to leave while Rose was upset with him.

She turned her attention to Charity. 'I told you to come away from that . . . person,' she said as sternly as she dared, her voice louder than usual. She paused, recovered her composure and then spoke more quietly. 'I hope you didn't speak to her, or she to you?'

'No,' Charity said.

'Or touch her – why, she might have had some terrible infectious disease for all we know, an old beggar person like that. You shouldn't be consorting with people like her.' Rose dropped her voice to a harsh whisper. 'If your father were to find out that Edward or I had let you near someone like that, we'd be in terrible trouble. We could lose our jobs and you would never see either of us again.'

'I'll never see you again anyway,' Charity burst out. 'Father is sending me away to school.'

This news came as a shock to Rose, and for a moment she and Charity stood on the cold white path staring at each other.

'Is that why you were crying?' Rose asked.

'Yes,' Charity whispered.

Rose opened her arms. 'Oh, you poor girl. Come here,' she said.

Charity tumbled, crying, against Rose, and Rose's arms folded close about her.

'I suppose it was bound to happen one day,' Rose whispered to her. 'You'll need to be brave.'

For some reason, thinking about leaving Stone Green Hall reminded Charity of what she had just learned. 'That old woman said she knew my mother,' she told Rose.

'She lives in a house in the woods over there. Some people say she's a witch,' Edward commented.

Rose turned to him, and when he saw her face, he quickly began walking back towards the house.

'The last thing young Miss Charity needs at the moment, Ned Cooper,' Rose called after him, 'is someone filling her head with stuff and nonsense about witches. Anyway, enough of all that now – let's think no more of it. Let me put this warm scarf on you, Miss Charity, before you go and catch a chill, or a fever, or worse.'

Charity allowed the wool scarf to be tied under her chin. 'I don't want to go away to school,' she said quietly.

'There will be other girls there of your own age, which will be nice for you,' Rose said. Then she added, 'I hope you didn't touch that old lady's hands, or give anything to her, or encourage her in any way. Promise me.' Her face was suddenly close and anxious.

'Of course not,' Charity said, sniffing back a tear and snuggling further into the scarf.

On the walk back to the house she thought about what the old lady had said regarding the horn and her birthday – and also just a bit about the nice chocolate she had given away. And then the news about her mother – who, it seemed, had not died giving birth to her at all.

Just what happened, then? she wondered. *And why would anyone lie to me about it – and why must I find the horn, whatever it is?*

Chapter Six

Charity was in the kitchen with Rose and Mrs Browne, the housekeeper and cook. She was sometimes allowed to eat her lunch there. It was a big, friendly room, a refuge from all the dark austerity around her. It was warm too, with the cooking range always on, and Mrs Browne would bustle to and fro in her apron, indulging Mr Tompkins every now and then with a little titbit of something that she was trimming or slicing. 'Greedy old puss. I don't know where he puts it all,' she would say admiringly.

Edward came in, his cheeks glowing from the

cold. He clapped his hands together. 'Mmmm, something smells good, Mrs Browne,' he said. 'I've been into town – to the chimney sweep, Mr Kawkins – and I'm frozen through.'

'It's lentil and bacon soup.' Mrs Browne sat down at the head of the table, facing the kitchen door. 'Good and warming.'

There were thick slices of rough brown bread too, and pats of bright yellow butter from the local farm.

'That old woman from the woods was out by the gates earlier today,' Edward said cheerfully between mouthfuls of soup. 'You know – the one they say is a witch.'

Charity pricked up her ears and tried to listen without appearing to.

'Now, now. That's not a nice way to talk about that poor soul, and you know it,' Mrs Browne said quietly.

'I know.' Edward looked slightly shame-faced. 'Some odd things do go on around here, though.

The master, for instance – did you know he goes walking around the house on his own, late at night?'

'Mr Delafield suffers from insomnia, Edward,' Rose muttered. 'And I think that's quite enough of that, don't you?' She looked over at Charity and nodded slightly.

Charity kept her eyes on her soup bowl as if she hadn't heard or noticed anything at all.

'Oh yes, of course. Sorry,' Edward said, and then added brightly, 'How was your morning, Mrs Browne?'

'Well, apart from it being so cold outside, and stirring up this great big saucepan of soup, and having to stay up late tonight to cook a batch of cakes I promised to the church hall – in my own time, mind—'

She stopped speaking mid-sentence and stood up suddenly, flustered, smoothing down her apron. Charity's father was standing tall and silent in the doorway.

'Sorry, Mr Delafield, sir,' the cook said. 'We were just—'

'Do not disturb yourselves. Carry on with your luncheon, please,' he said. 'I simply came to say that a visit from Mr Kawkins, the chimney sweep, has been arranged and confirmed for tomorrow morning at nine o'clock sharp, or so I gather from Edward. Therefore no fires are to be laid first thing. I also felt that I should share some news with you all. Miss Charity will finally be attending school before the coming summer. I think this news has perhaps upset her a little, given her sensitivity and her . . . condition.' He looked across the table to where Charity sat, as composed as she could manage, her face giving nothing away. She was used to hiding her feelings.

'In view of this,' he continued, 'I have decided to cancel this afternoon's ordinary lessons. Miss Rose, I suggest that calm, limited play may take place – within the confines of the house, of course.'

'Of course, sir, understood,' Rose said. 'Thank you, sir.'

'No need to thank me. Now, pray continue while your soup is hot – which, by the way, Mrs Browne, was excellent.'

'Thank you, sir. I shall collect the tray later.'

'Whenever it suits.'

And he left as quietly as he had arrived.

'Gave me a fair old fright, him standing there listening like that,' Mrs Browne said after he had gone. 'He had a glass of stout with his lunch today – for the iron, he said.' She winked at Edward, who looked over at Charity and shook his head.

'School for you, then, Miss Charity,' he said, smiling as sympathetically as he dared.

'Yes,' Charity said bravely, looking around the table at the friendly faces, and feeling Mr Tompkins underneath, curled comfortably at her feet.

'We have leave to play,' Rose said brightly, quickly changing the subject. 'After we have helped Mrs Browne to clear away, of course.

I think a game of hide-and-seek would be nice, don't you?'

'Good idea,' Edward said.

'What exactly is a game of hide-and-seek?' Charity asked.

'Well,' Rose began, always surprised by the number of ordinary playful things that poor, sheltered Charity knew nothing about, 'if there were two persons playing hide-and-seek, then one person – let us say, for the sake of argument, you – would hide away somewhere in a cupboard or the corner of a room, or indeed anywhere at all. The other person, eyes firmly closed, counts – let us say to a hundred – and then they come to look for you. When they have found you, if indeed they do find you, it is their turn to hide and yours to count and find, and so the game goes on. It is just a little harmless fun.'

The tall dark house was an ideal place for hide-and-seek. There were so many cupboards and hidden corners and long corridors. There were enough overstuffed and unused furnished rooms for several games. They began upstairs, so as not to disturb Charity's father while he worked in his study. Edward joined in too, and they drew playing cards to see who would hide first. He rigged the deck of cards nicely so that Charity won.

She left at once, walking quickly, getting as far away from the others as she could. Mr Tompkins followed her down the corridor. She opened the door to one of the smaller box rooms. It seemed a perfect place to hide. It was full of wooden crates and tea chests, piled up on top of one another, making a maze of pathways and spaces. Charity picked up Mr Tompkins and wriggled her way round, past the sharp corners of the crates, until she reached the back wall, and waited. It was cold in the box room and she was glad she had Mr Tompkins with her; he was warm to hold.

'They must have counted to a hundred by now,' she whispered in his ear.

The cat struggled gently and squeezed himself out of her arms, landing on the bare wooden boards with a soft *thump*. He walked off through the maze of tight spaces towards the door. Charity watched his tail flick past a crate. 'Come back,' she whispered.

She left her hiding place and followed him. He was sitting in a narrow space beside several tea chests which were stacked in a high tower. Charity wondered what was in all these crates. She could see bits of straw poking out of some of them, so she supposed they were full of china or glass. Mr Tompkins was rubbing against a particular crate. He stood on his rear legs and arched his back, then reached up with his front paws and patted at its open top.

'What are you doing?' Charity reached down and picked him up, so that he meowed softly.

The crate was out of alignment and part of the top was visible. Inside, she could see an envelope. She reached in carefully and took it out. Mr Tompkins meowed at her and touched the envelope with his paw.

'Shall I open it?' she said.

He meowed again.

She tore it open. There was nothing inside but an old key with an emerald-green ribbon tied through the end of it, as if it had once been fixed to a belt or key-ring.

She took the key and went back to the door. It did not fit into the keyhole. She opened the door and stepped outside into the corridor. She could hear Rose and Edward muttering and then giggling some way away.

'Time to find a new hiding place,' she said quietly to Mr Tompkins.

She crept further along the corridor, her heart beating fast. As she passed by one of the covered statues in a darkened alcove, she noticed that there was a door behind it.

She squeezed into the space at the back of the

statue and tried the key in the hidden door. It turned easily, but the door wouldn't open; then she looked up and noticed that a bolt was drawn across near the top. She reached up on tiptoe and slid it back. The door opened at once onto another long corridor. The walls were covered with green wallpaper, which was printed with such a dense pattern of leaves and branches that it looked almost as if it was part of a forest. She crept through and shut the door – and Mr Tompkins – behind her; the cat sat down to wait for her.

Charity saw that right beside her there was another door. She tried it and it opened stiffly, the bottom part scraping on the floor and making a low squealing noise. She went inside.

She found herself in a small nursery, meant for a baby. There was a cot covered with yellowed-looking white lace pillows and a patch-work blanket. The curtains were half-drawn, but she could see that the room was dusty and cob-webbed. It looked as if no one had been in there for a long time. There was something strange about it; something beyond its closed-off feeling and the intense cold and all the dust. Hanging from a brass ring in the ceiling there was a long green ribbon; and suspended from the ribbon, above the cot, was a large pair of rusty iron scissors; the sharp points were open, facing straight down at the musty pillows. She couldn't remember, or even imagine, being a little child and sleeping under that – and yet she felt she must have done. Why didn't she remember?

She bent down at the end of the cot under the hanging scissors. Something small and square was wrapped up in some pretty cotton fabric underneath. Charity pulled back a corner of the cloth and saw that it was a little book. Someone had wrapped it up as a present and then put it under the cot and forgotten it, or even tried to hide it. She unwrapped the book and opened it. On the first page was the title:

TALES OF THE ANCIENT ONES

edited & with an Introduction & Appendix

on the History of Faerie Lore

by A. Delafield

With Numerous Engraved Illustrations

Privately published by

Morris & Jones Ltd

The Unicorn Press

Chancery Lane

London

There was also a little piece of fine paper, folded once and tucked into the book. Charity opened it out and read:

Property of Ariella Delafield.
Stone Green Hall. & given with love to
her daughter Charity on this. the
Day of her Birth.

June 21st 1891

It had been written on her birthday too. On the day she was born, Charity's mother had been well enough to write that little message and tuck it into the book as a present. The old lady had been right. But if her mother hadn't died in childbirth, then what had happened to her, and when?

She heard the door opening behind her and quickly tucked the little book into her pinafore pocket. Rose came in on her own, muttering to herself, and so Charity popped up suddenly from behind the crib. 'You found me!' she exclaimed brightly.

'Oh, goodness me!' said Rose, her hand flying to her breast. 'You made me jump.'

'Did you count to a hundred properly? It should be your turn now, then,' Charity said.

Mr Tompkins padded in after Rose and rubbed against Charity's legs.

Rose looked around the room in wonder. She touched the cot and rocked it a little on its stand.

'Hush-a-bye baby,' she said quietly. 'However did you find your way in here? I saw Mr Tompkins waiting outside that door, and thought you must have come through it.'

'I found a key,' Charity said, 'and it opened the door to the corridor, and this door was open anyway. So I thought I'd come in here to hide.'

'I think you had better give me that key,' Rose said. 'This is the west wing, the closed-off and, I am afraid, forbidden wing of the house. It's kept locked because your father wants it that way, and I fear we must respect that.'

As Charity handed Rose the key she pointed up at the scissors hanging over the little crib. 'What do you think they are for?'

Rose looked up and saw the scissors on their ribbon, angling down at the baby's pillow like a threat, and a shiver went through her. 'I really have no idea,' she said.

Edward popped his flustered-looking head round the door, worry written all over his face.

'There you are,' he said. 'I think we'd better leave now. You may have found yourself a good hiding place, Miss Charity, and you win the game hands down, no question – but no one is allowed in here – not into the west wing, oh no,' he said in one headlong, breathless rush.

'It's all right, Edward. I've already explained that to Miss Charity, and we were just leaving,' Rose said. 'Miss Charity found an old key in the box room, and I have it now, for safe-keeping.' She held up the key on its emerald-green ribbon.

As they returned to the main part of the house, Charity picked up Mr Tompkins and held him in her arms. She could feel the weight of her mother's little book, her precious birthday gift, safely hidden and bouncing a little as she walked.

Chapter Seven

That night, as always, Rose brushed Charity's tangled hair before bed.

'Hold still, and it really won't hurt you,' she said. But it did hurt; it always hurt.

Charity said nothing more about the nursery they had found or what Rose might have done with the key to the west wing corridor. She would bide her time now; watch and wait. Her chance to explore would come. Strange things had happened today; inexplicable events had occurred. She would be alert from now on.

'There, all done now. Seventy-five strokes with

the brush, morning and night. That's the way, isn't it?' said Rose, almost as if to convince herself as she distractedly put down the brush. 'I'm sorry to always tug and pull, but your hair is so unruly, and Mr Delafield insists that it should be brushed properly.'

'Will you read to me?' Charity asked, and she casually handed Rose the little book she had found.

'Aren't you a little old for that?' Rose said, looking at the title. 'This morning it was an old spinning top, now it's fairy tales. What next? Going to sleep in a crib, no doubt!'

'Please?' Charity gave one of her rare and winning smiles.

'Come on, then, just for a while. But prayers first, then hands, then teeth, then only a very little reading.'

Charity knelt down by the bed with her hands clasped together. 'Bless Miss Rose, and Edward, and Mrs Browne, and keep them safe,' she gabbled automatically.

Rose said, 'You're forgetting your father.'

'Oh, of course, and bless Father too,' Charity added, not sorry to have forgotten him. 'And bless that poor old lady we saw, and keep her warm.'

'What did I say about that person before?' said Rose. 'Don't waste any blessings on her. Forget about her, or you'll be giving yourself bad dreams, if I'm any judge. Now, like I said: hands and teeth – no dreaming, and no dawdling.'

Mr Tompkins shadowed Charity along the dingy corridor to the bathroom, snaking around her feet as she walked. 'Come on, old puss,' she whispered. 'Don't let Rose see you.'

Before she reached the bathroom she slipped into Rose's bedroom. Sure enough, the little key on its strip of pretty green ribbon was hanging from the night stand. Charity tucked it into the pocket of her nightdress.

She washed her hands and brushed her teeth in the cold, white-tiled bathroom. She looked up at herself in the mirror, while the cat sat on the rim of the bath, licking his paws. She studied her neat, even teeth, and pulled her mouth wide open, staring at her pale face and her bright gold hair, hanging neat and straight.

Charity sometimes wondered exactly who she was, and where she had come from; what her mother had been like; and why she was always alone, like a well-cared-for prisoner. And what exactly *was* her condition? No one would ever tell her, even if she asked a direct question – which she knew she would never do now.

She just knew it.

She brushed her teeth with pale pink dentifrice paste. She spat all the pink out and raised her head again. She caught Mr Tompkins's eye in the mirror. The cat stared back at her, and she told him, 'We're going to explore the west wing later.'

Chapter Eight

Rose had been reading aloud for only a few minutes. The candle was burning low and their shadows flickered across the walls.

The first story in the book was about a fierce ogre and a young princess. The ogre was punishing the princess's father, the king, for hunting in his forest.

'The ogre turned the key, and the poor princess was locked away at once in the highest room in the highest tower in the high castle. The princess looked out of the narrow window. The wind blew fresh snowflakes past the window in a great flurry.'

Rose stopped reading. 'Sounds just like tonight,' she said, nodding at the window.

'It is,' Charity said, looking through the gap in her bedroom curtains at the swirling snow outside. Tucked inside her hand like a talisman was the tiny note left in the book by her mother, written for her on the day she was born. It was the only possession she had that she knew, for certain, her mother had touched.

'Go on,' she said, happily stroking Mr Tompkins's ears.

'Only to the bottom of this page, and then I'm stopping,' Rose told her. 'I can see you're sleepy.'

She continued reading:

'The princess tried the latch on the window, and after she'd pulled at it for a moment or two it gave way. The window opened, and a great rush of cold air and snowflakes filled the little chamber. She leaned out and looked down from the tower. It was a very long way to the tiny courtyard far below, and the princess

felt giddy just looking at it. She could see that, over the years, overgrown roses and gnarled old vines of ivy had climbed all the way up the tower. It was as if her prince had sent them in advance – a magical ladder to rescue her. She had no choice. She pushed herself out through the narrow space and prepared to climb all the way down the side of the tower. She would need all her courage.'

Rose shut the book. 'Well, that must be that, until the next time.' She smiled. 'I've read enough to you for now.'

'Oh no,' said Charity, 'but it's so cold for the poor princess.' She hugged warm Mr Tompkins and gave an exaggerated yawn.

'I shouldn't even have started this story,' Rose sighed. 'Your father would not approve of you digging out such childish things, and you know how much he dislikes fairy stories and magic and that sort of thing. It had better be our secret, all right? In any case, it really is time for sleep, and it's time for a certain cat to go out.' She lifted the uncomplaining Mr Tompkins down from the bed.

'Can't he stay in here with me? It's such a cold night, and it's snowing.'

'You know the rules as well as I do.'

'Please?' Charity said.

'I will leave your door very slightly ajar. If this naughty old cat comes creeping back in later, then that is up to him, and I shall take no blame for it. Goodnight now, Charity.'

'Goodnight, Rose.'

Charity waited what seemed like a very a long time for the house to settle. Gradually she heard doors closing and the hiss of gaslights being turned down. The house clocks struck the hours – nine, then ten, then eleven.

There was silence now. She sat up in bed and looked out of her window. It was still snowing. She felt Mr Tompkins nuzzle her legs.

'There you are,' she whispered. 'Come on, then – time to explore.'

Charity was almost reluctant to put one foot in front of the other. The corridor outside her room seemed so much colder, longer and darker at night, even though she could see clearly in the gloomy gaslight. She picked up Mr Tompkins and held him close. 'It's all right,' she whispered. 'Don't you worry.' She could feel his little heart beating as fast as her own. She put him down again, and set off.

There seemed to be even more of the dusty mounted animal heads than usual, their glassy eyes staring back at her from the shadows. She forced herself to walk towards the hidden door and the secret corridor. 'Come on, Mr Tompkins. You'll be all right. Just you stay close to me,' she said very quietly.

She finally found the door, still tucked away behind the statue in the alcove. She hadn't imagined it, after all – it really was there. This time she noticed that there were squares of green glass panelling with a pattern of leaves at the top of the door. Charity stood still for a moment, then pulled out the key on its green ribbon, placed it in the lock and turned it, before reaching up to slide the bolt back.

She went through into the green corridor, then locked the door behind her. It was very dark in the west wing. The furniture seemed to loom up among the leaves on the wall either side of her, as if she was lost in a deep wood. Beyond the nursery door were more doors. She counted two further on, both leading to the other forbidden rooms of the west wing. There were windows along the other side of the corridor, opening out onto the garden, and each window had long, green velvet curtains. Three sets were drawn across, but one was slightly open, letting in a thin strip of moonlight. She wondered if that meant it had stopped snowing.

If there had been long, fluttering muslin and

lace curtains instead of the green ones, Charity thought, then the corridor would have been identical to the one in her dream.

She didn't get as far as opening the door to the little nursery. The corridor was suddenly lit by a glow that shone through the glass panelling above the secret door. A lamp was moving closer, and she heard footsteps. She quickly hid in one of the many tall cupboards, draped with a dustsheet, but kept the door ajar so that she could see who was coming in behind her.

Charity heard a key turning in the lock, and lamplight spilled brightly along the corridor. A figure walked past. From where she was hiding she could see that it was her father. She held her breath. He was carrying a storm lantern and wearing his long winter cloak – the one edged with grey fur. Charity remembered what Edward and Rose had said about her father: that sometimes he didn't sleep, and would pace through the house at night.

Her father stopped. A black shadow was moving just in front of him. There was the slow flick of a black tail. Mr Tompkins turned and saw Charity's father standing in the gloom of the corridor, then arched his back and dashed off into the shadows, creeping under a chest of drawers so that only his green eyes could be seen.

'Go on, then,' said Mr Delafield. 'Spurn me again. I might as well have you stuffed and mounted along with all the others.' He gestured at the trophy heads on the walls. 'I should have shown you more affection when you were young; when I had the chance,' he said, in a surprisingly soft voice.

The cat blinked.

'What's the matter?' Charity's father murmured, bending down to peer into the dark space. 'Cat got your tongue?' He laughed to himself and went further along the corridor.

Charity stayed very still, and watched. She

could not remember ever having heard her father speak in that tone of voice before. He was always so stern and correct with her, and even more so with poor Mr Tompkins.

Mr Delafield stood the lantern on top of a dustsheeted bureau, then reached up and pulled a great swathe of cloth away from something large and rectangular hanging on the wall.

It was a painting in an ornate gilt frame. At first it was so dark that Charity couldn't see the image on the canvas at all. Then her father picked up the lantern and held it close to the picture.

It was a portrait of a young woman. She had hair just like Charity's; it was the same fiery golden colour, and it tumbled in loose waves around her pale shoulders. The woman had been painted against a background of summer trees and she was wearing a dress of green velvet. To Charity she looked very beautiful – she had a slightly amused smile which suggested someone playful; someone who liked to laugh and tease.

For a moment Charity's father stood in silence in front of the picture. Then he sighed, and Charity distinctly heard a sob.

There were twelve tings of a brass bell, as a clock somewhere in the house chimed out the midnight hour.

At that, her father spoke. 'Happy birthday,' he said, quietly and sadly.

Then he put the lantern down again and the picture went dark. He pulled the dustsheet back over the frame and tucked it into place before calling out to Mr Tompkins, 'Come on, then, you silly old cat, or I'll lock you in.'

The cat trotted out from under the chest of drawers. Charity's father swept past her hiding place, and Mr Tompkins followed along behind.

She heard the door being opened, a pause, and then it closed again. She heard the key turn in the lock – and then the bolt being drawn across. The spill of light from the lantern swept away. The corridor grew dark again, and somehow colder too.

Charity clambered out of the cupboard. She listened to the silence of the house. It was the witching hour, and she was standing on her own in a long, unknown dark corridor. She shivered and rubbed her goose-pimpled arms. Even Mr Tompkins had gone.

She went over to one of the high windows and pulled the curtain further aside so that some cold snowy light came in from the garden. Then she went over to the picture. She reached up and tugged the corner of the dustsheet away.

She stared up at the lovely smiling face and the tumbling rush of wild, golden hair. She had never seen a picture of this woman before, but she knew exactly who she was; she seemed to call to Charity out of the quiet darkness. Charity's eyes travelled down from her face to her throat, where a necklace caught her eye. It was made of big green stones that matched the dress. There was a label on the bottom of the frame – a name printed in neat black capital letters. '*Ariella Delafield*,' she read out slowly. She gazed up at the smiling face of her mother. 'And it's your birthday today too. I never knew that. And I never knew what you looked like, either. So that is you.'

Time ticked by in the shadowy, leafy-green gloom of the corridor while Charity looked at her mother – the mother she had never known. Finally, before she tucked the dustsheet back over the painting, she said, 'Goodnight, and happy birthday from me – and from Mr Tompkins too, if he was here.'

She tiptoed back to the door, hoping against hope that she wasn't trapped in the west wing. She put her key in the lock, feeling it turn, then tried to open the door, but her father had indeed bolted it on the other side. She put the key back in her pocket.

She tried the nursery door. It opened after a little shove, and she found herself facing the baby cot and the hanging scissors. There was just enough moonlight breaking through the snow clouds to enable her to see. She rocked the little cradle back and forth in the near dark, and imagined the woman in the picture standing here, rocking it and singing a lullaby. She tried to remember hearing the soothing voice of her mother as she sang. She imagined that she could hear the sweet voice now.

Suddenly Charity thought she heard music nearby – but not a lullaby. She opened the nursery door and listened. She hadn't imagined it – a very faint melody was coming from somewhere further along the corridor. It sounded like a waltz tune. She followed the music past two more doors. It seemed to be coming from within the leaf-covered wall itself. She shivered. Then the music stopped and there was silence again, apart from the wind whistling around the chimneys.

Although it had been beautiful, the music had frightened her and she quickly returned to the nursery. Once the door was closed she listened again for any music, but there was no sound apart from the creaking floor boards as she walked.

She noticed that just over the nursery door there were words painted on the wall. Someone had written ONCE UPON A TIME, and had decorated the letters with twisting tendrils, leaves and roses, like the walls of the green corridor. Rearing up in the middle of it all was a beautiful white horse. No, it wasn't a horse . . . it was a unicorn. Charity wondered if her mother had had it painted for her. '*Once upon a time,*' she said out loud.

She had to get back to her own bedroom, and soon, but the door that led back through the house was bolted. She looked out of the window: the moon was hidden by cloud again, and the snow was whirling and spilling past the leaded panes of glass.

I'm just like that princess in the story, she thought. She opened the window, and cold air rushed in, along with some driven flakes of snow. She looked down and just managed to make out the thick trunks of old ivy and roses twisting up the wall.

'The princess climbed down,' Charity said to herself. 'She was brave. Perhaps I can be brave too.'

There was so much snow falling now that she could hardly see the ground, but at least the wind seemed to have dropped. It was certainly very quiet, and no one would see her – they would all be in bed by now. She looked left towards the other windows – three more of them, staring darkly and blankly at the garden. Luckily the branches were at their thickest under the old nursery window.

Charity dared herself to climb up onto the windowsill. She balanced on the sill, and felt each tingling flake of snow as it landed on her.

She had no idea whether the branches would support her. There was only one way to find out. She sat on the sill and dangled her legs over the edge, and then lowered one foot and pressed down on a branch. It felt springy but firm. She turned round awkwardly on the sill and allowed her legs to drop behind her. She gradually lowered herself further, holding tightly onto the sill.

Then, finally, she summoned all her courage and let go.

Chapter Nine

The first branch supported her foot enough, so she lowered the other one to join it, grasping the tangled stems of ivy with her hands. She stood balanced on the thick wet branch and dared herself to bounce just a little, testing the wood.

It held.

She felt about with one leg. Her cold feet found another branch lower down, and she settled on that one, and then gradually the next, as if she were climbing down a set of very large and very far-apart stairs, and all without being able to see where she was going.

'*Once*,' she said out loud to herself as she worked her way down.

'*Upon*,' she added, feeling with her toes and clinging as best she could onto the cold slippery branches.

'*A*,' she continued, daring to look down.

'*Time*,' she finally whispered, seeing how far she still had to go to reach the ground.

She hadn't even thought of how she might get back into the house. 'If a made-up princess in a story can do it, then I can do it too,' she said aloud, as if reassuring herself. Then something occurred to her. *I am in my own fairy tale*, she thought as she balanced on another gnarled old branch of climbing rose.

She looked up through the gently drifting snow at the line of windows above her, all four of them dark and empty-looking, and she shivered – partly from cold, and partly from the loneliness of that hidden corridor. The dark, forbidden west wing . . . But *why* was it forbidden?

She made slow progress, but she could sense the ground getting nearer. When at last she looked down again, it was very close and thickly covered with snow. She let go and jumped the last few feet. She stood shivering, with the snow almost up to her knees, and looked at the main door of the house. She knew for certain that it would be locked and bolted now.

Hugging herself to keep warm, she dashed across the snow-covered garden, away from the west wing, towards the back of the house. There was a light burning in the kitchen window. Charity peeped in and saw Mrs Browne at the table, still awake and finishing off the cakes she had promised to make for the church hall. She opened the back door as quietly as she could and waited in the little vestibule near the boot rack and the umbrella stand. The iron radiator was still warm to the touch and she pressed her feet against it, one after the other. It felt so good that she sighed out loud, and Mrs Browne popped her head round the kitchen door.

'Whatever are you doing out here, Miss Charity?' she said. 'Come on in before you catch your death!'

The kitchen was even warmer and smelled of baking. Mrs Browne put the back of her floury hand against Charity's cheek. 'My, you're like ice,' she said. 'Whatever were you up to out of bed at this time of night?'

'I don't know,' Charity said. 'I must have been sleepwalking, I think.'

'I'll make you a nice warm drink. How about a cup of hot chocolate? And not a word to anyone, mind,' said Mrs Browne. 'I have a secret tin of chocolate powder in the cupboard. Little weakness of mine.' She pressed her finger to her lips and winked.

Charity put both hands around the cup as she drank. She felt the sweet warmth coursing through her.

Mrs Browne took Charity back up to her

bedroom using the serving staircase that connected the kitchen with the rest of the house. Mr Tompkins was sitting outside Charity's bedroom door and he followed them in.

Mrs Browne tucked Charity up in bed. 'Just you go back to sleep, now, and I don't want to see you up again until morning. I shall have to tell Miss Rose about your sleepwalking, I'm afraid.'

'I'll tell her,' Charity said quickly.

'And I'll tell her as well,' Mrs Browne insisted, 'and I expect your father will have to know too.'

She turned off the light and closed the door. Charity felt herself warming through at last as she burrowed under the heavy blankets. She closed her eyes and listened. The house was quiet, and if the snow was still falling, it made no noise. All she could hear was Mr Tompkins purring at the end of the bed.

'I did it,' she whispered to herself. 'I found her. I saw my mother for the first time and I had an adventure. I climbed all that way down in the dark on my own, like the princess in that story.'

In her dream she was back in the green corridor in the west wing. The wind was blowing the lace curtains away from each of the windows so that they fluttered and billowed across the floor. The branches on the wallpaper moved too, and the leaves rustled and shifted in the wind.

Charity followed Mr Tompkins along the corridor. The cat stopped at a section of wall. Charity put down her candle carefully. The waltz music was coming from somewhere, very softly, and the cat put his head close to the wall as if he were listening to it.

'Please let me in. I want to go to the ball and dance,' he said.

'I can't,' Charity told him. 'There is no door.'

'Oh,' said Mr Tompkins. 'Of course there is a door. You just have to find it.'

Chapter Ten

Charity was woken by Mr Tompkins pulling at her bedcovers. Rose came in, looking tight-lipped. She shooed the cat out and then closed the door.

'Whatever were you thinking of last night?' she said, without a trace of a smile.

'Thinking of . . . ?' Charity got out of bed and played for time.

'Mrs Browne tells me that she found you sleep-walking. The key to the west wing was gone from my night stand when I looked this morning.'

'It's here,' Charity said, fishing it out of her

nightdress pocket and handing it back to Rose.

'You weren't sleepwalking, were you?'

'No,' Charity admitted, avoiding Rose's eye, looking instead at the whiteness of the fresh snow outside. 'I just wanted to explore that old nursery, but I got locked in the west wing. So I climbed down the wall from the window.'

Rose took Charity by the shoulders. 'What you did was very dangerous. You could have caught your death of cold – or, worse, fallen from so high up. What on earth possessed you?'

'I wanted to find out more about my mother,' Charity explained. 'There was a painting of her in the corridor, all covered up.'

'I don't know much about your poor mother,' Rose said. 'What I do know is that she is sadly dead, and that your father does not want us going into the west wing. He has his reasons, whatever they may be, and we must respect them.'

'I saw him there last night,' Charity told her.

Rose hesitated. 'Well, it's a very good job he didn't see you – that's all I can say.'

'It's snowed again.'

'I know it has, miss, and don't think you can just change the subject and then no one will say any more about it. If your father finds out about this, he is very likely to send you away to that school – that institution – earlier than he planned, and you wouldn't want that.'

Charity said nothing. She looked suitably chastened and crestfallen.

'I'm afraid there will be no fire in here, nor anywhere else in the house, until after the sweep has been,' Rose continued brightly. 'So make sure you wrap up warmly. I am serving your breakfast in the nursery today – at least there's the oil stove in there. Now, promise me you won't go poking around where you shouldn't any more, as I have to go out later.'

'I promise,' Charity said. 'I should like to watch the sweep work, though,' she added.

Rose shook her head. 'Mr Delafield says you are to stay safely in the nursery today, for a sweep's work is very dirty work indeed.'

Charity ate her breakfast on her own in the warm nursery. She let Mr Tompkins lick some milk from the saucer, then gently shooed him out into the corridor. He meowed outside the door for a moment, then stopped, and she imagined he had wandered off.

The clock began to chime the hour.

From the nursery window Charity could see Edward walking down the path to the main gates. He had no shovel today – just a big ring of keys in his hand. She watched him unlock the padlock, unfasten the chains and pull hard to open the great iron gates.

A covered tradesman's cart rolled along the twisting road from the town, pulled by a black horse. There was something written along the side panels, but Charity couldn't read it through the blur of the black railings. The cart slowed down near the open gates. She could just see the shape of a man sitting high up in the driving seat. Then it slowed and turned into the driveway, straight through the open gates, the driver hidden by the canvas cover. Just then the clock finished chiming nine.

The wagon rolled round to the back of the house. Charity could finally read what was painted on the side, in white letters on the black cloth:

ISAAC KAWKINS ESQ.
CHIMNEY SWEEP

Chapter Eleven

Rose had carefully laid out Charity's arithmetic lessons for the day on the nursery desk. There was also a book which Charity dreaded seeing. It was bound in dark red cloth and the label stuck on the cover read: RAY'S INTELLECTUAL ARITHMETIC: 2ND VOLUME FOR ADVANCED STUDENTS.

Rose had already chosen a page of problems, and Charity's exercise book was open. Her pen and pencils were lined up in the groove at the top of the sloping desk.

Charity's heart sank. She hated problems.

They always dealt with things about which she knew nothing: trains passing each other at different speeds, farmers filling grain sacks, bankers weighing coins.

She opened the book and read the first problem:

A gentleman left his elder daughter £1,500 more than his younger, whose fortune was £11,111. What was the elder sister's fortune and how much did the father leave them in total?

Charity groaned out loud and covered her eyes with her hands. She tried to think about the two sisters and the father and the money, but she couldn't. Some other problem was worrying away at her, and, like her dream, it was just out of reach. It was something to do with numbers, anyway . . . Had she dreamed that too?

Her thoughts were interrupted by a sudden noise, like something heavy rolling across the ceiling. Then a great storm cloud of black soot rolled out of the cold nursery fireplace. Charity stood up quickly and stepped back against the window.

There was a loud *thump* as something fell into the blackness, and then whatever it was started to climb up out of the fireplace. The cloud of dust settled around the figure of a thin boy of about her own age.

His soot-blackened face was split at once by a bright white smile. 'Sorry, miss,' he said. 'Bit of loose brickwork.' He pointed up at the chimney breast. 'Hazard of the job.'

Charity stood there, dazed, staring at the shabby, blackened apparition in front of her.

'I'm Silas, miss. Silas Jones, sweep's boy, at your service,' he went on. 'Foundling, sold on at the age of seven from the parish to the care and apprenticeship of Mr Isaac Kawkins, chimney sweep. He's all right, I suppose – he drinks a bit now and then, if you know what I mean. I tell you something – he had to light fires under me at first to get me to go up the chimneys.' The boy shook his head, as if at an unhappy memory. 'I was named for the Welsh woman who found me on the workhouse doorstep, and I'm pleased to know you, miss.'

'Do you really go up chimneys all day long?' Charity asked.

'Certainly do,' he said. 'I wish I didn't have to, of course, but then it's another world up there amongst all the flues and chimneys. You'd be surprised what you can find. Hidden things. Treasures even, sometimes.'

Silas made to step forward, but only got as far the brass fender. 'Better not go any further,' he said, looking down at himself and the soot. 'This is a big house you've got,' he added, nodding his head, so that soot fell from his messy hair back into the fireplace. 'Lots of very old, top-quality wide chimneys. You all on your own in here, then? Looks like a schoolroom – I seen one once.'

'Yes,' said Charity nervously. 'Just me. I never go out or see anyone. I've never even met a boy before.'

'What – never ever?'

'No.'

'So let me get this straight. Here you are, a girl all on her own, more or less locked in, just like a prisoner in a tower? Like the one in that story – the girl with lots of hair?'

'You mean Rapunzel?' Charity said.

'That's her,' the boy replied. 'I don't expect you're her, are you? What might your name be, then?'

'I'm called Charity. Charity Delafield.'

'Nice to meet you, miss,' Silas said. 'Seems a shame, you shut in here all day. And you've got no friends at all, then?'

'Not one. Well, there's my cat, and the staff here. They're nice to me, but my father won't let me meet anyone else to be friends with.'

'Why's that, then?'

Charity hesitated. 'He says I have a condition.'

'Is it catching?' Silas said with a wide grin.

'No.' Charity cast her eyes down to the carpet.

'I didn't mean to upset you. Just my idea of a joke – sorry. Maybe I could be your friend? Your condition wouldn't bother me.'

'I don't see how we can be friends,' Charity said. 'I'm not allowed out.'

'Then I'll come and see you. I have my little ways of getting in and out of anywhere. Don't you worry, I'll manage.'

Silas reached his blackened hand out towards Charity, who took it carefully. 'Friends?' he said.

'Friends,' she agreed, looking at the black smuts on her hand.

'The lady and the sweep's boy,' he added, another friendly grin spreading across his face.

There was the sound of the door handle turning, then the nursery door opened and Mr Tompkins came in. He was followed by a tall man dressed in a tattered, old-fashioned black coat, with a high top hat on his head. The man's face was blackened over with soot, but his eyes were pale and stared straight at Charity.

'Apologies,' the sweep said in a rasping voice. 'I had no wish to startle you, miss. I know we must both look quite a sight, all covered in the old black stuff as we are, but I was looking for 'im.' He nodded to Silas and pulled an empty sack from under his coat. 'Here's a sack for you, lad,' he said, handing it across. 'Now, you might clear up this unseemly mess. Sad to say, he does this a lot, miss. He will explore when he's in the chimneys – does more than he should – and then, as you see, these messy accidents will happen.' He produced a little black lacquer dustpan and a matching japanned brush, and gave them to Silas.

'This is very fine house, a very fine house indeed,' Mr Kawkins commented. 'Very old too. I've worked here before, you know, some years ago now. Cleaned everything through from top to bottom for the lady of the house.'

'The lady?' Charity stared.

'She would have been your mother, I'm judging, from your hair colouring and your demeanour. You're very like her. She was a most striking individual.'

'I never knew her,' Charity told him.

'Like me,' said Silas, crouched in the fireplace. 'I never knew my mum, neither.'

'More sweeping, lad, less talking,' Mr Kawkins said. 'People remarked on her beauty too,' he continued. 'Known for it, she was, about these parts. A rare thing.' He sighed and shook his head, then turned to Silas. 'Are you done, lad? Let me see . . . I don't want to see a speck, mind, not a speck.'

Mr Kawkins bent down and examined the hearth, then ran his hand in its mitten across the nursery rug and examined the tips of his fingers.

'All right, lad, let's get you back to work. Forgive the intrusion, miss,' he said, doffing his battered top hat.

'Very nice to make your acquaintance, miss,' Silas said as Mr Kawkins ushered him out.

'I would like to think that we might meet again,' Charity said quietly, and Silas winked back at her as the door closed.

Chapter Twelve

Later, the sweep's wagon rattled out between the iron gates. Charity watched from the nursery as Edward padlocked the chains back in place behind it. He stood there and shivered, and then looked up at her window and waved. The black wagon rolled away, out along the road, past the forest, taking her new friend with it. She watched it as far as the first bend in the road, and she wondered if she would ever see Silas's bright, impish smile again.

She finished the maths problems as best she could, and Rose came in to mark them.

'I made a friend,' Charity said.

'A friend? Really?' Rose's pen paused, and she looked up. 'Who?'

'Silas,' Charity told her.

'Who is Silas?' Rose asked.

'The boy helping the chimney sweep,' Charity explained.

'How did you meet him?'

'He fell down into my fireplace.' Charity smiled to herself at the memory of it.

'I see,' Rose said. 'I don't think your father would react well to you being friendly with a dirty sweep's boy.'

'He couldn't help being dirty,' Charity protested. 'It's his job. You'd be dirty too, if you had to go up the chimney.'

'I would, but luckily I don't have to, and neither do you.'

Charity looked out of the window while Rose continued checking the problems. *There's something about the windows on the west wing. Something odd . . .*

she thought. It troubled her in some way, but she couldn't think why.

Rose turned to her and said, 'If you want to stay on your father's good side, I would pay more attention to your work and less to boys who fall down chimneys. I can't see any working out for these answers, miss. I think you just guessed them.'

'They make my head hurt,' Charity muttered.

'I know they're difficult, but they just require logical thought and concentration – qualities that your father is very keen for you to develop.'

'Is that why he is sending me away to school?' asked Charity sadly.

'Believe me, I know how you feel,' Rose said gently. 'My own school days were not easy. But they gave me certain skills, and I have reached my position through hard work and using those skills. For someone like you, anything should be possible.'

'I shall marry a prince,' Charity told her.

'Oh, will you? And where will you find this prince?'

'In a palace, of course.'

'Some would see this house as a palace.' Rose looked around at the fine solid furnishings and the rocking horse and the high ceiling.

'Well, it's big enough,' Charity said quickly, and then, in a rush, she added, 'But there are no princes here, are there? Unless Edward is secretly a prince and is in hiding from an enchanter who is going to cast a spell to stop him marrying the secret hidden princess.'

Rose blushed, but quickly collected herself and said, 'There you are, you see. This is what your father means. It's just that kind of thing he can't stand – these flights of fancy of yours.' She sighed. 'I think you had better try these problems again, Miss Charity.'

When Rose had gone, Charity left the nursery, followed by Mr Tompkins. She crept past the bathroom back to the box room that had been her first hiding place in the game of hide-and-seek, when she had found the key hidden in the old tea chest. This time she tried the door next to it, and it opened easily. It was dark inside – the heavy curtains were drawn across the window and the Holland blinds were lowered too. Chairs were neatly stacked up, four or five high. There were few gaps in the piles of furniture.

Mr Tompkins mewed and vanished among a jumble of sheeted chairs and furniture.

'So many things,' Charity said aloud. 'Just like in that other box room . . . Why is it all hidden away, I wonder?'

She pushed between the dusty piles. 'Where are you, Mr Tompkins, you naughty old cat?' she muttered.

There was a narrow gap over to the window, where a pale strip of light was shining on the wooden floor. Charity squeezed her way through, past rows of tall cupboards. She noticed that one cupboard door was half-open, out of line with the rest. She stopped to reach through the gap in the door and felt around. She came across hard, smooth objects – vases or glass bottles – wrapped in pieces of tissue paper.

She pulled one of them out. It was a china cup. Even in the half-light she could see that it was an oddly dark colour, a kind of deep velvet green. There was a roundel on the side of it, and in the roundel was an image of Stone Green Hall. She held it up and turned it in her fingers. Under the picture of the house was a little swag of leaves and roses with the shape of a heart in the middle. She wondered why she had never seen this china used at tea time.

She put it carefully back with the others and reached in again, finding something on one of the lower shelves – clearly a book. She pulled it out, then squeezed herself over to the window, lifting the edge of the Holland blind and balancing it on the arm of one of the covered chairs so that a little more cold daylight seeped into the room.

The book was bound in soft green suede – the same colour as the cup. The green had run in places, as if the book had been soaked in water and had dried out again at some point. It was very small, and had one word stamped on the cover in patched and faded silver: DIARY.

Charity sat down on the cold floor. Mr Tompkins found her and curled up on her lap. She opened the book.

There was no name, and no clue as to who had owned the diary. The paper was very thin – even thinner than the paper in Rose's prayer book. It smelled wonderful too – not as she had expected, seeing as it was so water-damaged: the scent that rose from its pages was both sweet and light, in contrast to the musty old books in her father's library; like the honeysuckle that grew on the trellis of the kitchen garden. Charity closed her eyes and breathed it in, and she almost felt warm again.

The first few pages had clearly got so wet that the writing had blurred and run; she couldn't read it. She turned the pages very carefully, because the paper was crinkled and very fine and she was worried that she might tear it. Several pages in, the blurry water stains stopped and there was an entry in perfect tiny handwriting. It filled the whole page in neat, straight lines. The writing reminded her of something. She held the book closer and tried to read what was written.

Saturday

Mother tried to calm me. 'Don't take it to heart,' she said. 'Father means no harm. He is conscious of our special traditions, and does not want to see you making a mortal mistake. He loves you, that is all.' I wish I could believe her. I am so unhappy – but I will be with him soon. That will make me happy – I know I am doing the right thing.

Charity realized with a start that the tiny words she had just read had started to rise up off the page like smoke, and vanish into thin air. She stopped reading and closed the little book. In a state of shock, she stared at the mottled, damaged green suede cover and the patchy silver lettering. How was this possible? She dared not open the book again for fear all the words would blow away. Was it some special kind of ink that had dried to dust, or was it the operation of something else . . . a kind of magic?

She was keen to show it to someone – but not Rose. Who? She would show it to Silas, that was who – her new friend. She tucked the diary back onto the shelf for now, and carried Mr Tompkins out of the room.

'That book was magic, I know it,' she whispered in his ear. 'Magic.'

Chapter Thirteen

In the dream she was walking along the green corridor again. The leaves on the wallpaper looked very bright, and shifted in the wind. It felt warm, like summer. Mr Tompkins was walking ahead of her, and he was as tall as her, and walking upright on his hind legs, which seemed perfectly normal. They reached a door at the furthest, darkest and narrowest end of the corridor. Bright, inviting light glowed through the gaps where the big brass hinges were, and through the crack under the door too. Waltz music was playing in a whirling rush, and Charity felt an urge to go into the room and dance. She turned the handle but the door was locked. She rattled it and tried to push it open.

Mr Tompkins was leaning against the door jamb, looking down at his claws, flexing and blowing on them. 'I told you there was a door,' he said.

'I want to go in,' Charity announced.

'Well, you'll need a key. That's the trick.' Mr Tompkins looked up at her with his big green eyes.

Charity sat straight up in bed. It had been the old dream . . . but different. How had it been different? She tried to grab hold of it in her memory, but it dissolved like the words written in the diary, and slipped away. She looked down at the end of the bed where Mr Tompkins lay curled at her feet. 'You were standing up – I remember that,' she said.

She went down to the kitchen.

Mrs Browne smiled when she saw Charity and gestured for her to come through into the scullery. This was a small, cosy room beyond the kitchen, where Mrs Browne kept all the best china – along with her own special ornaments and souvenirs that people had brought back from the seaside for her. Charity always liked going into the scullery; it was like a secret treasure trove with all the shiny copper pans, china jugs and trinkets.

Mrs Browne said, 'I've got something for you – just a moment.'

Charity looked along the shelf of seaside souvenirs. There was a white china mermaid with a bright green glittery stripe on her tail; she remembered Mrs Browne letting her play with it when she was little – very carefully, of course. There was a little china boot with a picture of Worthing on it, and behind that a small piece of weathered wood with traces of white paint, twisted like a piece of barley sugar. Charity remembered that from long ago, too, and something made her reach out and pick it up and tuck it quickly into her pinafore-dress pocket. She couldn't explain why she had done so – she just felt she needed to.

Mrs Browne came back from the cold store. She held out a smudged envelope. There was no stamp, and on the front, in carefully lettered script, was written: *Miss Charity*.

'This letter was tucked in next to the milk churns this morning,' Mrs Browne said. 'Good job *I* went to the gates to bring them in, and not someone else – someone a bit stricter. It seems you have a friend somewhere. I should tuck that away and keep it to yourself if I were you.' She gave Charity a conspiratorial smile.

Charity said nothing in reply, but she smiled back. She took the letter and put it in her pocket, next to the little twist of wood.

She was eating breakfast with Mrs Browne when Edward popped his head round the door.

'It'll be me taking you for a walk this morning,' he said, winking and patting his jacket pocket.

Charity frowned at first, and then realized what he meant – chocolate.

That made her think. She had given her last secret treat away to the old lady at the gate. She wondered if she might see her again – and, with luck, it might be *after* she had managed to eat her chocolate this time.

They stayed on the paths near the house, away from the clipped trees and the statues, which were all safe from the cold under their sacking covers. Mr Tompkins ran along beside them on the cleared stone flags. When they were out of sight of the front of the house and were skirting the east wing, Edward reached into his pocket and pulled out the few squares of chocolate in their gold wrapping. Charity stood still, unwrapped one and allowed it to sit for a moment in her mouth and melt.

'Good?' Edward asked.

'Mmm,' she said, smiling.

'Glad to hear it.' Then he added casually, 'So, does Rose ever mention me at all . . . you know, in conversation?'

'Sometimes,' Charity said through a mouthful of warm chocolate.

'Oh, and does she speak well of me?'

'She is always very polite.' Charity was savouring the chocolate.

'Oh, polite . . . I see,' Edward said. He stood looking for a moment over towards the trees and nodded to himself.

Charity finally swallowed the chocolate and ran on ahead, chased by Mr Tompkins.

'Not too far now,' Edward called out, walking slowly behind her, lost in thought.

Charity turned the corner in a rush. Now she was at the back of the house, and she was careful to keep out of sight of any windows. She quickly tucked herself in amongst the snow-dappled ivy, then took the envelope out of her pocket and opened it. The piece of paper inside had ISAAC KAWKINS ESQ. & APPRENTICE, FOR ALL YOUR FIREPLACE AND CHIMNEY NEEDS printed in bold black letters across the top.

Below that was written in a clumsy but earnest hand:

Nice to meet you miss. Meet me tonight after nine o'clock near the big gates, if you can.
Yours truly,
Silas Jones
Apprentice Sweep

Charity crumpled up the letter and put it in her coat pocket. Edward sauntered round the corner, blowing on his hands, and spotted her at once, half hidden amongst the ivy.

'I should come out of there, Miss Charity, if I were you. It must be very cold in all that wet greenery.'

'I was enjoying the chocolate,' she said,

popping another square into her mouth and savouring it. 'Thank you so much,' she added, and smiled. She was enjoying something else too – another layer of secrecy: a time and a place to meet her new friend.

'Sit still now, and it won't hurt,' Rose said.

It would hurt, though, and she knew it, but Charity was prepared for it, used to it, and in any case she felt stoical tonight. Just knowing that she was going to sneak out of the house later to meet Silas somehow made her feel strong, and a little fearless. She sat up straight as Rose pulled the brush down through her long golden hair, and she did not flinch.

'You *are* being good,' Rose said.

'Will you read to me?' Charity asked.

'I see.' Rose gave a wry smile. 'That's why you're being good and brave about the brushing. That's what's called cupboard love.'

'I like you reading to me.'

117

'And I like reading to you,' Rose said, 'but isn't there something a bit more grown up you ought to be reading? Something more scientific?'

'I like these stories,' Charity said, settling back against the pillow. Hidden under the covers, she held the precious note from her mother tightly in her hand. She also held the little twist of worn wood she had taken from the scullery; she liked the feel of the warm soft wood against her skin. She imagined Mrs Browne had found it on a beach on holiday when she was a girl, and had just kept it.

Rose began reading:

'Once upon a time and a long time ago, there was a young princess. She lived with her father, the king, in a fine palace. She had kindly servants to look after her, and she was happy enough, or so she thought. Then, one summer morning, she was out early, hunting in the forest with her father, when her horse struck a boy with his hooves and knocked him down. The boy

lay on the ground, and at first he seemed to be dead.

'The princess was sorry for what she had done. She begged her father to let her take the boy back to the palace to see if the royal doctor could help him. The king was reluctant. "He is but a peasant boy, and no concern of ours," he said. But the princess insisted that it was her fault, so the boy was brought back to the palace.

'"He is perhaps more shocked than hurt," the palace doctor said, "but he will need time to get better properly."

'The boy was kept away from the princess while he recovered from his injuries, but she found ways to visit him secretly, and they soon became friends.'

Before the story came to an end, Charity was already snuggled down and fast asleep. Rose closed the little book. She looked down at the girl with her golden hair spread out across the pillow. It would soon be tangled again after the night. In the morning it would need all that painful brushing once more.

She put down the book, tugged the bedcovers into place, and shooed Mr Tompkins out into the corridor, where he sat looking up at her with his green eyes.

Chapter Fourteen

Charity wasn't really asleep at all. She lay with her eyes tightly closed, almost believing that she *was*. She was in that odd half-awake state – the strange place where she often found herself early in the mornings.

She had been thinking about her mother and the painting in the corridor. She could see the beautiful face so clearly, and as she looked, her mother's mouth twitched upwards at the corners and smiled at her. She quickly sat up in bed. Suddenly something was absolutely clear to her.

The diary. She knew who the diary had belonged to.

But for now, she had to meet Silas. Heart racing, she put a warm coat on over her nightdress, slipped on her boots and crept out of her bedroom, along the corridor to the back stairs. She walked past the cases of stuffed animals, and this time their glass eyes catching the light didn't frighten her.

She tiptoed past the closed kitchen door and quietly let herself out into the cold. She hurried along the path towards the gates, ignoring the looming statues wrapped in their sinister sacking, and the creaking evergreens rustling in the night wind.

At the gate she could see the moon in the distance. It cast a silvery light onto the road and the trees and the banked-up snow. Silas was waiting on the other side of the railings, his breath misting in the moonlight.

'Have you been waiting here long?' Charity asked.

'Not very long, miss,' he said. 'I'd rather be out here in the night air than up a chimney, anyway. Shall I climb over now?'

'Be careful . . .' Charity looked back at the darkened house. 'The railings are sharp.'

'It's all right, miss,' Silas said. 'I've got this.' He waved an old soot sack at her and shimmied up the railings. He laid the thick sacking across the sharp tops of the railings and scrambled over, landing in the snow.

Charity looked up at the sack, still draped across the railings, and pointed at it.

''S all right, miss, I'll need it for getting back over later. I won't leave it there, I promise,' Silas told her.

'I've got something to show you,' Charity said.

'Where, miss?'

'In the house – and please call me Charity. We're friends now.'

'All right, miss.'

'We *are* friends, aren't we?'

'I hope so . . .' Silas said, hesitating. He almost added 'miss', but stopped himself. 'Charity.'

'Good. Come on, then – quickly and quietly now.'

From the kitchen they crossed into the main hallway, and Silas immediately went across to the big fireplace.

'I could go everywhere in the house from here, I reckon,' he said, his teeth shining white, 'and back again too.'

'Not now,' Charity said. 'Follow me, no talking. Come on up the stairs.'

Mr Tompkins emerged from the shadows and padded along behind them.

Charity took Silas along the corridor past the bathroom. The gaslights were turned low but they could see their way clearly. She took him to the box room with the piled-up furniture looming under the dustsheets.

'Look at all this stuff!' Silas exclaimed.

'There's lots more,' Charity told him. She

pulled the little green diary out of the cupboard where she had left it. 'I want to show you something very special,' she said quietly. 'We need to go into the light.'

They went back out into the corridor and stood under the nearest gas mantle, which burned with a cold, greenish flame. Mr Tompkins sat near the door that led to the west wing, and stared back at them.

'This is a diary kept by my mother,' Charity told Silas. 'I am going to open it and show you a page; just watch very closely.'

She opened the book to the first blurred, water-stained page.

'Can't make it out,' Silas said, staring hard.

'I know . . . wait.'

She turned the pages over until she reached one with writing on it. As they tried to read the small, neat words, they seemed to dissolve off the page into the air in front of them.

'You see what's happening?' Charity said.

Silas stepped back and looked up into the gaslight, trying to follow the progress of the smoky letters as they left the page. 'It's magic,' he said, astonished.

'I know,' Charity murmured.

'Look!' he said. 'It's going back in there.' He pointed to the half-open door of the box room. The thin line of almost-invisible smoke drifting off the page was curling itself into the room.

Silas turned to follow it. Charity closed the diary and went after him, with Mr Tompkins behind her. They pushed their way through the piled-up furniture, watching the line of whitish smoke as it slowly floated towards the fireplace. Mr Tompkins started meowing.

'It's gone up the chimney,' Silas realized.

'I'll never be able to read what she wrote,' Charity said sadly.

'You just have to read it quickly,' he suggested helpfully.

'I want to be able to read it more than once,

though,' she said. 'It was written by my mother –
it's the only thing I have of hers, and it speaks to
me: it can tell me about her, and how she felt. How
does it happen, anyway – what makes the words
drift off the pages like that?'

'It's a spell. I reckon it's old magic from the
ancients,' Silas told her. 'Mr Kawkins was telling
me about her.'

'About who?' asked Charity.

'Your mother. It was on the way back from
cleaning the chimneys. He said he remembered
the big party they had here for her wedding. She
invited all the villagers, and the strange folk from
the forest, and there were Chinese lanterns in the
trees, and fireworks.'

'Fireworks?' Charity found it hard to imagine
her father allowing fireworks, let alone inviting all
the villagers and the forest folk – whoever they
were – to the house.

'Lovely fireworks, he said they were – magical.
And he said there was real magic there too.

It scared some of the villagers. You wouldn't want to cross them – wild people, you know, the ancient folk.'

Charity held the diary close to her heart. She didn't want to open it again for fear of losing more of the words inside. 'No, I don't know,' she said. 'Who are they?'

'Like I said, the ancient ones. The folk from the forest.'

'Ancient ones? Do you mean old people?'

'No, I mean the old time people.' Silas glanced around and whispered, 'The ancient ones – you know . . . the *faerie*.'

'Fairy people?' Charity said, her eyes widening. 'You mean they're real?'

'Kawkins says they've been in the forest for years and years. The village is superstitious about them, worried about curses and spells.'

'Do you believe him?' A sense of recognition stole over Charity and caused her to shiver. 'Only, I've found some strange things in this house,' she added. 'There is an old nursery with a crib, and hanging over the crib there's a pair of sharp iron scissors pointing down.'

'Do you think that's to do with the ancients?' Silas asked.

Charity didn't answer because there was a sudden noise from the corridor. Mr Tompkins scuttled away as if he had been scalded. Charity tucked the diary into her pocket.

'Someone's coming. They mustn't find us,' she whispered, and she pulled the box-room door shut with a click. She waited, pressed against the door, and motioned to Silas to hide himself.

'I can get out through the chimneys,' he called back softly. 'Don't you worry, miss – I mean, Charity.' He set off across the dark room, swung himself up inside the chimney where the words had gone, and disappeared.

Charity imagined it was Rose looking for her, and then she heard Mr Tompkins outside, scratch-ing at the door and meowing. The footsteps were louder now. A man's footsteps. Edward? She tried to shush the cat through the thick oak of the door, but it was no good. Mr Tompkins kept up his plaintive noises, and the footsteps stopped outside the box room. Charity moved away from the door and stood stock still.

She heard a voice: 'Oh, it's you. I might have known it. Prowling about in the dark, eh? What sort of mouse have you got locked up in there, you silly creature?'

The box-room door opened and the gaslight spilled in from the corridor. Charity was revealed, standing perfectly still in her winter coat. Mr Tompkins trotted in and rubbed himself against her legs.

'What on earth . . . ?' Her father's voice was quietly shocked. 'Are you sick, child? What is this? Why do you have your coat on?'

Charity stayed very still, partly out of fear, and partly because she thought she might pretend she was sleepwalking if she stayed in a still, dreamlike state. She simply stared ahead, looking through the shadowy shape of her father looming in the doorway. It was the first time she had consciously deceived him in any way.

He walked into the room and stood in front of her. 'Whatever is happening?' he shouted angrily, and Charity also sensed something else – a terrible fear in him. 'You have no idea of the danger you could be in, wandering alone in these corridors unsupervised! Have you gone completely mad? I don't want to lose you too . . . Answer me, child!'

She stood with her hands straight at her sides, ignoring even Mr Tompkins, who continued to curl around her feet, meowing softly.

'What on earth has come over you, my girl?' Mr Delafield said, just a little more quietly. He shooed Mr Tompkins away with a clap of his hands and then stood looking at her from the doorway for a moment. 'Are you ill? Your eyes are open, but you don't respond . . . If you are tricking me, it is not at all funny. You are in the gravest danger, and yet you have no idea . . .' He was trembling.

'I must fetch Miss Rose,' he whispered, and closed the door.

Charity stayed where she was. Her father's reaction had both puzzled and scared her. She called out quietly into the darkness: 'Are you still there, Silas?'

There was no reply. She supposed he must have climbed all the way up the chimney.

It was not long before there was a commotion outside. Two voices, and then the door swung open again.

Rose came in. She was wearing her dressing gown. She reached a hand forward very gently and touched Charity on the shoulder. Charity stared straight ahead. She didn't know what else to do.

'She is dressed as if she is going outside,' her father said. 'Something in her condition has suddenly worsened. This is something I have always feared, ever since she was a baby. I knew this day would come. A doctor must be fetched, and soon – it is a matter of life and death.'

'I wouldn't go that far, sir . . .' Rose ventured. 'It is quite common, I believe, for girls of Miss Charity's age to sleepwalk in this way. We must take her carefully back to her bedroom and do our best not to wake her – I have read that it is possible to induce a seizure of the heart if you wake a sleepwalker.'

'Is that what you believe this is?' Mr Delafield asked. 'Sleepwalking? I fear it is something much more sinister.'

Charity allowed herself to be taken by the hand and coaxed out of the room. She moved forward with little steps, and her hair flickered gold every time they passed into the glow of one of the gaslights. Her father winced every time, and looked at her anxiously.

'It is clear to me, Rose, that she must be locked in her room at night for her own safety,' he said. 'Either that, or you will have to share sleeping quarters with her – and even that may not be safe enough.'

'It seems drastic, to lock a poor child in, sir . . .' Rose said.

'This is a drastic condition, Rose, believe me. I have seen its like before. There is real danger here. A lock and key – that's the only answer.'

Back in Charity's bedroom, Rose took the girl's coat from her shoulders and slipped her shoes off. 'Her feet are like ice,' she murmured.

'She'll soon warm through once she is in bed,' Mr Delafield said.

Charity allowed herself to be helped back under the blankets, and she opened and closed her eyes slowly, as if still in a dream. She prayed that Rose and her father would leave her alone now.

Rose folded the coat and laid it across the arm of a chair. The little green diary fell out, and landed on the floor with a thump. Charity turned her head slightly – just enough to see her father bend down and pick it up.

'What's this?' He flipped through the first few pages.

'I have never seen it before, sir,' Rose replied.

Charity's father examined the pages a little further into the diary. 'Oh no . . .' he whispered.

Charity heard Rose give a cry of astonishment, and by turning her head a little further she was able to see the thin trail – the smoke of the letters, her mother's precious words – flying off the pages as they were turned. Charity was powerless to stop it – she knew she had to keep up the pretence of sleep.

'Whatever is happening?' Rose asked.

'It is just the dirt and dust from an old, empty book,' Mr Delafield told her. 'An unused diary from a few years ago, of no interest to anyone.' After he had flicked through all the pages and the smoke and dust had drifted away, he put the book away in his pocket.

'Lock the door when you leave, Rose, and bring the child to me in the morning.'

Chapter Fifteen

Charity heard the door click shut, and then the key was quickly turned in the lock. She lay staring up at the darkened ceiling for what seemed like hours. She had seen her mother's precious words float out of the book and vanish like smoke up the chimney, and now she would never be able to read what had been written there – even though she was sure that it had been meant for her.

It seemed as if the little book was under some sort of spell. Was it to protect what her mother had written from prying eyes? But why would she have to do that? And why had her father not appeared the least bit surprised to see the words floating off the page? He had quickly explained it away to Rose – it was almost as if he had expected it to happen.

Charity reached her hand out, but there was no Mr Tompkins, and no soft ears to stroke. He was locked out, along with everyone else. She worried about Silas too, vanishing like that – but then he was used to climbing chimneys and exploring, and she assumed he had managed to get away.

She finally drifted off to sleep as the house settled down around her.

In her dream she was in the green corridor again, and a bright light was shining through the leaves. The music was playing behind one of the doors, but no matter how fast she ran towards it, the door never got any closer. This time she was all on her own – there was no sign of Mr Tompkins anywhere.

In the morning Rose brushed Charity's fine gold hair seventy-five times. Mr Tompkins sat on the bed, licking his paws and watching Charity with his green eyes. It hurt more than usual, and Charity had to hold herself rigid as the silver-backed brush pulled down through the tangled strands. She curled her toes tightly, clenched her teeth and pressed her fingernails into her palms, until that hurt more than the brushing.

'Very tangled this morning,' Rose said. 'You've got it into a terrible pickle. I'm sorry if it's hurting.'

In the looking glass Charity smiled back at Rose as best she could.

Rose shook her head and sighed. 'Your father is very worried about you. He found you in the middle of the night standing in one of the old box rooms, as if you were half awake and half asleep. He was very, very agitated and alarmed, and sent for me, and I said I thought you had been sleepwalking. He wants to see you in his study this morning, which I why I am taking extra care with your hair. Seventy-two . . . nearly there.'

Charity steeled herself. The brush plunged through her hair three more times and then Rose put it down on the glass top of the dressing table.

Charity put on her plain grey wool day dress and a white pinafore. Rose tied a pretty emerald-green ribbon loosely in her hair and matched it with another wider velvet ribbon of the same colour around her neck.

'There,' she said. 'Let me look at you.'

In the glass, Charity caught a glimpse of herself. She could see a sudden and clear likeness to the covered portrait of her mother that waited to be unveiled again.

Mr Delafield was sitting at his desk, poised and serious. He had his back to them, but as she and Rose came in, Charity thought he seemed unusually agitated.

'What is that around your neck, child?' he asked at once, turning to look at her.

'A ribbon, Father, that is all.'

'It matches the one in her hair, Mr Delafield,' Rose explained. 'I thought that—'

He cut Rose off. 'Remove them, Miss Rose – immediately. They are both gaudy and unnecessary. My daughter is still a child, after all.'

'Certainly, sir. I am sorry – I had no idea it would offend you so.'

Rose took the ribbon out of Charity's hair and then undid the one around her neck. She draped them over her arm.

'There is something wrong, something unsuitable to my eye about that colour. I do not blame you, Miss Rose, in any way. You were trying to present your charge at her best, which is just as it should be. Your attention to detail does you credit; you were not to know that I do not care for that particular shade.'

Mr Delafield took a moment to compose

himself before continuing. 'You may stay with us, Miss Rose,' he said. 'I would like you to hear what I have to say, and to confirm all this.'

Rose closed the door against Mr Tompkins, who had followed them down the stairs, then took a seat at the side of the room.

'Sit yourself down, child,' Charity's father told her. He waited while she settled, and then stood and paced to and fro in front of his desk while he spoke.

'Late last night, when walking along the corridor on the top floor, I found that wretched cat of yours meowing and scratching at a closed door. I thought that perhaps for once it had been of some use and caught a rat, or some other vermin. Imagine my dismay when I opened the door to discover my own daughter, wearing an outdoor coat and boots in the middle of the night, standing alone in a dark, cold, closed-off box room! I fetched Miss Rose at once, who told me that this sort of thing is quite common.

Has anything like this happened to you before, child? Tell me honestly.'

Charity shook her head. 'I don't know, Father. I cannot remember, I am sure. I do have vivid dreams sometimes, in which I am walking.'

'Dreams are just fragments and patterns,' he replied, 'made by the sleeping brain. They have no more meaning than the cold rocks of the planets and stars that surround us. A dream will not make you walk. I am afraid this is another manifestation of your sad condition – the legacy of your poor mother.'

Charity's heart leaped. Her father had never before mentioned that her 'condition' was something she had shared with – and directly inherited from – her mother. It was the first time he had referred to them both together. 'Did my mother walk in her sleep too?' she asked curiously.

'Never mind that now, child. As far as I am concerned, sleepwalking is a danger to the sleeper and to the rational mind. It can be fatal to wake a sleepwalker, which is why Miss Rose and I had to guide you so carefully back to your bed. If nothing else, you could have developed pneumonia standing there in that cold room. What possessed you to take an old empty diary out of a cupboard and then just stand there? Have you no memory of doing any of it at all?'

'None, sir,' Charity said quietly.

'And yet your eyes were open, wide open. It was most strange and unsettling, if not alarming. And there is another thing.'

'Another thing, sir . . . ?' Rose said with an anxious look on her face.

'Yes, Rose, there is another thing, about which you are not expected to know. Edward found a set of footprints leading from the house to the railings and back again. It seems that someone might have broken into the house. This worries me more than anything else. It is even possible that this intruder was with you, alongside you, Charity. Do you know who it was?'

Charity met her father's gaze levelly. Just a few short weeks ago she might have looked down at her feet or traced the complex patterns in the Turkish carpet with her eyes – anything rather than look back at him when he was speaking to her like this. Now things had changed. She had a friend in Silas, and she knew things – secret things. She was watchful, she had been brave, and she was gradually uncovering something that had been kept from her since she was a baby. She would not be intimidated.

'I was asleep, Father,' she said politely. 'I didn't see anyone come into the house, and I don't remember being outside at all. Surely the cold would have woken me if I had gone outside?'

Mr Delafield shook his head. 'Not necessarily. Sleepwalking – or somnambulism, to give it its rational and scientific name – is a strange condition. The sufferer may carry out both ordinary and dangerous tasks without being remotely aware of them. I would hate to think that some criminal element such as a burglar might have exploited your condition in order to steal things from the house.'

He stopped pacing and stood beside his desk. 'I am afraid that new restrictions will have to be imposed. I have already written to the institution I mentioned to you. I have brought forward your starting date.' He held up a cream-coloured envelope with his wax seal freshly impressed on the back. 'At least there you will be properly and safely monitored by an experienced medical staff.'

'I thought it was a school, Father,' Charity said, horrified, 'not a hospital.'

'It is a scientific institution, Charity, where you will learn. But you may also be observed, because of your condition.'

Charity bit her lip. She would say nothing further. Nor would she show her true feelings – her agonized dismay at what she had just heard. She glanced at Rose, who looked worried herself.

Mr Delafield nodded at Rose. 'I will speak to

Miss Rose shortly about the new restrictions that will have to be put in place until you leave for the institution. Edward and Mrs Browne have already been informed. No one is to be in any doubt as to the seriousness of this . . .' He hesitated as if searching for the right word. '*Invasion*,' he said finally. 'The usual level of supervision must be increased, plus there will now be extra security at night. I have engaged the services of a retired soldier to patrol the perimeters of the house until such time as you leave here to start your studies, Charity. We must all take special care of you now, my poor child. All this is for your own protection, believe me.'

Charity was sent to the kitchen. Mrs Browne called her over to her side of the broad wooden table. 'Come here, dear, just for a moment.'

She immediately folded Charity into her big bosom and squeezed her tight. 'There, there. Mr Delafield told me earlier, and I can imagine how you must be feeling. We are all looking out for you, Miss Charity,' she added quietly. 'He means well, and he only has your best interests at heart, but sometimes – well, I won't say it, but you know you can always be assured of our support. Now, I shouldn't be telling you this, but there was another note this morning. It was tucked between the milk churns again. I hid it from your father when he was in here earlier. Make sure you hide it well or burn it after you've read it, won't you?'

Charity drew back from Mrs Browne's friendly embrace. Eyes shining, she sniffed and took the envelope. 'I will,' she said, and put it in her pocket.

'Breakfast for you, I think,' Mrs Browne said.

Later, Charity shut herself in the bathroom and opened the envelope.

Dear Charity,
I made my way back through the chimneys, over the roof and down. I found something you will not believe. Now it

will be my turn to show you something special. I will come
whenever I can. Soon, I hope. Be ready.
Your friend,
Silas

How was she supposed to be ready? Silas wasn't to know that she would be locked in at night from now on – and how could she tell him?

She folded up his note very small, went to her room and tucked it between two books in the bookcase. Rose was waiting for her in the nursery.

For the rest of the day Charity sat at her desk and worked diligently at the maths and science problems. Although they were still tedious, she somehow felt above them now. She could keep them in a neat compartment in her head while the rest of her mind soared upwards in her imagination.

Things were adding up – and not in the same way as the maths problems. She had read some of the stories in the fairytale book, and they seemed to be meant for her, as if someone, somehow, had intended for her to read them and recognize the clues and links between the events in the stories and those in her own life. She had also seen glimpses of her mother's diary – and the portrait of her mother. She had met the old midwife who had been present at her own birth, and she had made a brave friend, who in turn made *her* feel brave. And there was one other thing that she was sure of too, though she hardly liked to even think of that. She would only let that thought into the darkest and wildest part of her mind at night, in the pitch black of her bedroom, just before sleep, when there was no chance of it escaping. Then, and only then, could she hug the secret thought to herself with a deep certainty.

That night Rose handed Charity the little book of fairy tales.

'I think you might read to yourself tonight.

I will be down in the kitchen with the others. I'll come in and check on you later.'

'Where is Mr Tompkins?' asked Charity. 'Can't I have him with me?'

'Your father wants you sleeping properly, so no old pusscat to disturb you, I'm afraid. Goodnight, now. Sweet dreams – and I mean just that.'

Rose turned the key in the door so that Charity was firmly locked in.

Charity picked up the fairy tale book and turned to the next story: *The Princess in the Dark Wood*. She felt sure that she had to read the stories in the order in which they appeared in the book – any looking ahead might break the spell, if that is what it was. It certainly felt as if there was something odd and rather magical happening.

Once upon a time, there was a princess who lived in a royal castle, close to a big dark wood. Her mother, the queen, went out one morning to gather mushrooms, which she liked to do before the sunrise, when they were still wet with dew. She would carry them back in her shawl, which would sparkle with bright water droplets in the early sun. Except for this one morning, when she didn't come back at all.

The king sent his knights out to find her, but there was no trace of her anywhere – except for her abandoned shawl.

The princess was very upset. She felt that her father had given up on finding the queen too quickly. The princess was good friends with the boy who groomed the horses in the stables, and she arranged for him to have a horse ready for her early the next morning. She intended to go and look for her mother herself. She was not one to give up on anything.

She stole out early on the fine white horse, just like her mother, before the sun had even risen. She rode deep in amongst the trees.

In the darkest part of the wood, where hardly any sunlight penetrated through the dense branches and leaves, she saw something pale attached to a tree trunk. She rode nearer and saw that it was a piece of thin paper, torn from *a book. There was writing on the paper, and it was in her mother's hand. She moved closer to read it – when the wind suddenly blew it up into the air and tumbled it over and over, just out of reach.*

Charity put the book down. 'Like the words in the diary,' she said to herself. She laid her head down on the pillow. 'The words that vanished off the page, just like in that story.'

She closed her eyes and quickly fell into a deep and, for once, dreamless sleep.

Something was touching her face; a gentle tapping. Mr Tompkins's paws, she thought. She reached out through the solid darkness and touched something she wasn't expecting.

A hand.

She was awake and stifling a scream in an instant. There was a glow of fizzing yellow light which lit up a face. It was Silas. His finger was pressed against his lips and he was covered in soot.

'Shhh,' he said. 'Don't worry, it's only me.'

'I can see that,' Charity said, breathing more steadily now. 'You *did* frighten me. I thought you were going to be my cat, Mr Tompkins.'

'I sent you a note.'

'I know you did. What is it you need to show me that's so very urgent?'

'You'll thank me when you see,' Silas said, grinning.

'That is not an answer. Besides, I can't go any-where. I'm locked in, because they think I was sleepwalking, so you'll have to bring it to me, whatever it is.'

'I can't,' Silas said. 'You must come with me.'

'How am I supposed to do that?' Charity asked.

'Simple. We'll go up the chimney.'

Charity stared at him. 'Are you mad, Silas? I can't go up a chimney.'

'You can – it's easy. The chimneys in this house are wide and well-made, you'll see. And I'll be there to look after you.'

'Can't you get into another room and then come and unlock this one and let me out?'

'No,' Silas replied firmly. 'You have to come with me. It's the only way – you'll see what I mean.'

Charity hopped out of bed. 'It'll be filthy up there,' she said.

'You might have to give your face a once-over with a flannel,' he admitted, 'but it'll be worth it – really it will. Look, just follow me. Once we get beyond the chimney breast you'll see why.'

Silas shone the lamp into the chimney and climbed up. After a moment his head reappeared, lit from above by the lamp so that he seemed to have a halo. 'Come on,' he said. 'Take my hand and I'll help you.'

Charity stepped into the fireplace and shut her eyes. The ash and cinders crunched together, still slightly warm under her feet. She reached her arms forward and felt herself being pulled upwards. She was scraped against the chimney breast, and she coughed at the dust.

'Open your eyes,' Silas said.

Charity opened them. Silas had set her down on a wide ledge inside the chimney. He sat on the opposite side, holding the lamp high above his head so that the light shone around the space above them.

'Take a minute,' he said. 'Let your eyes get used to it.'

She blinked a couple of times and looked up at the rough, blackened brick insides of the chimney. 'Well?'

'Don't you see it?' Silas asked.

She squinted, and then saw a faint pattern scattered across the layers of soot. She looked more closely and realized that there were letters and words carefully inscribed in white amongst the black.

'Writing?' she said.

'Yes, writing.' Silas pointed to the chimney walls. 'All through the chimney system – words, everywhere.'

Charity swivelled round on the ledge and leaned forward. She read out loud from the lines closest to her head '. . . *And all is agreed and prepared at last, and my mortal love and I will be married and will live at his fine house not far from my kind, and I shall be with child . . .*'

She sat back, her heart racing. She suddenly understood what this meant. 'It's a miracle,' she said.

'It really is,' Silas agreed. 'That first day I met you, the first time I was in this chimney system, none of this was here. The walls were black, simple plain black. No writing of any kind.'

'You know what this is?' Charity said.

He shook his head. 'No.'

'It's the writing from that little book I showed you. The diary written by my mother. Those words that burned off the page like smoke . . . this is what happened to them. They floated up here and wrote themselves on the chimney walls.'

Charity knelt quickly and read some more from a section higher up: '*I will wear a dress of springtime green and ribbons of a darker hue, of forest and of emerald. My folk will brush my hair over and over until it shines, for I must look my best for what is to come . . .*'

'I knew you had to see it,' Silas said, grinning.

'Oh, you are clever to notice it. I was so upset to think that I had lost all those words – that they had faded away like dust. I know she wanted me to read all this – I just know it.'

'I'm sure you're right.' Silas tapped the lamp gently. 'Light's about to go out, and you won't like it up here in the dark. We'd better go back to your room.'

'No – please,' Charity said. 'Let me read some more – just a few more words.'

'The lamp will fail at any moment,' Silas told her.

'Just one or two more . . .' She turned her head and greedily drank in another phrase from the soot around her. '*We are caught between two worlds, that is our problem. Our love is a bridge between them, but can it support us?*'

The lamp went out and the two of them sat for a moment in the cold darkness.

Silas was the first to move. 'I'll go down first, then I can help you. Don't worry.'

'I'm not worrying,' Charity said, but as if to convince herself.

Silas slipped down from the ledge back into the fireplace. 'Here,' he said. 'Let me find your feet.'

Charity felt his hands close around them.

'I've got you now . . . Ease yourself down, I'll support you.'

She felt his arms grasp her knees as she lowered herself down out of the darkness. They stood in the fireplace, smiling at each other, both covered in soot.

'Mr Kawkins told me something else about this house,' Silas said, as if he had just remembered. 'You remember you told me there was a pair of old iron scissors over the crib in that nursery? Well, Mr Kawkins said they was hung over cribs in the old days to keep away the ancients. Stopped 'em stealing babies, he said. They didn't like iron – they feared it and stayed away.'

'That doesn't make any sense, really,' Charity said. 'My father wouldn't believe in anything like that.'

'Maybe your mother did, though—'

There was a tap at the door. They both froze.

'Are you all right in there, miss? I thought I heard voices.' It was Edward, and he was turning the key in the lock.

'I'm going,' Silas said, as quietly as he could, and began to climb back up the chimney.

'Ask Mr Kawkins some more about her,' Charity whispered.

'I will,' he promised, and then he was gone.

The door opened a crack, and light from the lamp in Edward's hand spilled into the room. Charity was lit up where she stood, just in front of the fireplace. Her eyes were open but she feigned sleep.

Wondering what Edward would say when he saw the mess, her eyes flicked down. With a shock she realized that the soot had all disappeared. Her nightdress was as white as snow, and her hair shining gold; she looked as if she had just stepped out of the bath.

Edward stood looking at her for a moment. The orders had been clear: they were to keep an eye on things, but on no account were they to wake the child. There was no one else in the room, and no sign of any disturbance. Edward assumed Charity had been talking to herself. He walked into the room as quietly as he could and rested the lamp on the chest of drawers, then took something out of his pocket and tucked it under Charity's pillow. At the same time Mr Tompkins, unnoticed, slipped in from the corridor like a shadow and crept under the bed.

Edward didn't want to touch Charity, or speak

to her, but he did think she should get back into bed. He thought of waking Rose, which cheered him briefly, but he dared not. So he picked up the lamp and left the room, leaving Charity alone.

Charity heard the click as the key turned again. She opened the curtains and looked down at her hands in the silvery light from outside. They were perfectly clean. She lifted her feet up onto the windowsill one by one; they were pale and clean too. She didn't understand. Like Cinderella, she had stepped in the old ash in the grate, and she had been pulled up and down inside the dirty chimney – yet there was no trace of soot on her. She suddenly remembered Mr Kawkins running his hand over the rug after Silas had cleaned up with the little lacquer dustpan and brush, looking for any telltale trace of soot. There had been none then, and there was none now. Had Silas somehow managed to clean everything in the dark without her noticing?

Impossible.

She shivered, and then slipped back into bed and laid her head on the pillow. So many things would have seemed impossible only a week ago.

She felt the crackle of gold foil under the pillow, and pulled out the four squares of chocolate that Edward had put there. She unwrapped a square and let it sit on her tongue, feeling it melt sweetly and slowly in her mouth. There was a soft *thump* as Mr Tompkins jumped up onto the end of her bed, purring softly. His comfortable weight settled on her cold feet, and then his paws began pulling at the bedcover as if he were kneading dough for bread, just like Mrs Browne did in the kitchen.

Charity had a lot to think about. It was so strange knowing that she had her mother's diary after all – only now it was written in white against the black soot of the chimneys, and spread all through the house in a long secret letter – a letter that was meant only for her.

Chapter Sixteen

Rose brushed Charity's hair as she sat at the mirror.

'It is much warmer this morning. All that snow is finally melting,' she told her.

It was true. Charity had lain awake listening to the drips before Rose had even unlocked the door.

'Edward told me he heard you talking to yourself last night, and he came in and found you standing by your bed, fast asleep.'

'Did he?' Charity tried to look as surprised as she could.

'He hasn't said anything to Mr Delafield about it yet, and I doubt he will. As long as you were in your room you were safe enough.'

Charity thought of sitting up in the chimney with Silas, reading the secret words written all over the sooty walls. If only they knew.

After breakfast Rose took Charity out for a quick walk around the house. Mr Tompkins walked with them, avoiding the wet patches of melting snow. Edward was out too, but instead of clearing the paths he was climbing a stepladder beside one of the statues. Charity noticed that the sacking around it had come away. Edward was now unwrapping the statue, checking to see if it had been damaged by the frost. Charity had never taken much notice of what exactly the statues were meant to be, or what characters they represented. They were just the statues in the garden. As this one was unwrapped in the bright morning sunshine, she suddenly looked at it differently and wondered whether it might be telling a story.

She stopped beside it, and saw that it was a woman with a bow and a quiver of arrows. A young deer stood beside her. 'Who is that?' she asked.

'Why, Miss Charity,' Rose said, 'if you were to use your eyes, you would see that there is a bronze plaque close to your feet, which might answer your question.'

Charity read the inscription. '*Diana the Huntress*,' she said out loud.

'You remember her, surely?' Rose said. 'We read about her a long time ago, in that book of mythology . . .' She paused and shook her head slightly. 'Before your father took it away, that is. She was the beautiful daughter of Zeus, and she hunted and lived with the animals in the forest.'

'Yes, I do remember,' Charity said, looking up at the face of the statue. 'How long have these statues been here?'

'Oh, I don't know. A long time, I should think.'

'From before my father bought the house?'

'I couldn't say,' Rose said. 'Come on – it may be thawing, but it's not exactly warm.'

They carried on round the west wing of the house. Charity looked up at the row of four blank windows that stared dully down at the garden, and at the scrabble of twisted stems and branches that clung to the walls up to the window ledges. She thought, *I climbed all the way down from there. It looks much higher in the daylight than it did in the dark.*

Later on, Charity watched Edward from her window when she was meant to be working. He was now wrapping the statue of Diana in sacking once more.

If she had stayed at the window just a little longer, she would have seen the old lady again, standing outside the gates. The woman called out to Edward, but he waved her away and turned his back on her, then walked back up the path towards the house. The old lady pushed some-thing through the bars of the gate – an envelope. It fell into one of the last drifts of snow, un-noticed, white on white. Then she turned away, her shoulders slumped, and headed back across the road and into the trees, where she vanished amongst the dark trunks and branches.

At bedtime, after the hair-brushing and bath-room and prayers, Charity was once again locked in. She sat up in bed and picked up the fairy tale book. She turned to the next story, forgetting that she had not yet finished the one before, and resisted peeping ahead. This one was called *The Hunter*. She was over halfway through the book now. The right-hand wodge of pages was thinner than the left. The stories would soon be running out.

Once upon a time, there was a young woman of the ancient kind who lived with her family in the forest.

The trees stretched for miles in every direction, as far as the eye could see. Mortal folk often hunted or foraged there, but they rarely saw the ancient ones, who kept themselves to themselves.

Wild deer roamed the forest, and many other kinds of beast too. There was even the rarest of them all: the unicorn. Only the ancients were allowed to see the unicorn. Mortals tried to find it and hunt it, but they never succeeded, so the ancient folk tolerated their presence and let them be.

The image of the unicorn again. Charity thought back to the snowy spinning top, and the painting of the unicorn above the door of the old nursery, surrounded by roses and leaves. She felt sure that this wasn't a coincidence.

She put down the book and hopped out of bed, then went over to the window and looked over to the big forest beyond the railings. It was very close to the edge of the garden, but she had never been there. She could imagine it all clearly.

There would be twisted branches and dense leaves overhead, making it dark even on the brightest day in summer. And she knew that there would be all kinds of secret things growing amongst the tree roots in the gloom. She had seen pictures of them in botany books: mushrooms and toadstools clinging to the sides of trees, all spongy and slimy looking. Were the ancients, whoever they were, living in the forest now?

Another thought occurred to Charity. If the ancients were still living in the forest, did it mean that the old lady was one of them?

She got back under the covers and carried on reading.

One winter morning, a rich young man from a fine mansion was out hunting, alone on his horse. It was barely daylight and it was still dark under the dense canopy of leaves and branches. He saw something out of the corner of his eye – a flash of white moving through the trees. He thought it was a white hart, and followed it on foot, taking just his bow and quiver.

In the middle of the forest he came to a pond and saw the fine white creature, drinking with its head bowed. When it lifted its head, the huntsman saw a single horn growing from its forehead. This was no deer, after all.

The young huntsman hid among the bushes. That unicorn will be my finest prize; the best of all my trophies, *he thought. He raised his bow, took aim and loosed his arrow.*

At that moment he realized that the unicorn was not alone. A beautiful girl stood next to it. She had golden hair that tumbled down over her shoulders and seemed to glow with an inner light against the dark background of trees. As the arrow flew towards the unicorn, the girl tried to throw herself in front of the creature, for she knew there was no crime more terrible than to harm one of these rare and magical beasts.

She was too late. The hunter's arrow grazed her arm, but struck the unicorn with full force, and the creature's horn was broken off. It reared up on its hind legs in terror and galloped away into the forest. The hunter wanted to run away too, but something compelled him to stay with the girl, who now lay among the cold leaves.

As he walked towards her, he noticed how oddly she was dressed. He now realized that she was one of the fabled ancient ones. He looked down into her beautiful eyes, brimming with tears and colours and reflections. Her fine green dress was slightly torn where the arrow had caught her arm, and her pale skin bore a red weal. When he reached down and touched her, her skin was like nothing he had ever felt before.

'I am so sorry,' he said. 'I did not intend to hurt you.'

'I know,' she replied. 'But you do not understand what you have done.'

The girl explained to the hunter the severity of his crime. She knew that if the rest of her people found out what he had done, the consequences for him would be grave. But despite his folly, she had been struck by

another arrow in those few brief minutes, and the pair
fell quickly and deeply in love . . .

Charity looked up. She had heard a scrabbling noise from the fireplace. A pair of black boots dropped down from the chimney, attached to a pair of skinny legs. Then Silas appeared, grinning his friendly grin, with a bag slung across his back.

'I said I'd return to you soon,' he told her.

'How did you manage to get in?' Charity asked. 'Edward found your footprints in the snow and my father thought an intruder had tried to break in. Now he has hired someone to patrol the fence all night – an old soldier.'

'I know.' Silas nodded. 'I saw him marching up and down, but he didn't see me. I just waited till he was out of sight, then hopped over and up onto the roof. Easy.'

Charity jumped from her bed. 'I want to read some more of my mother's diary up the chimneys.'

'I thought you might. I've got a better light with me this time – a proper chimney light. I borrowed it from old Kawkins – not that he knows, mind.' Silas pulled a copper lantern out of his bag and pumped a little nozzle up and down. Soon the lantern glowed with a bright, even light. 'Come on, then,' he said.

Charity climbed after him into the chimney, following the trail of words in the soot, stopping every so often to read more. Silas diligently held the lamp up for her while she read. She raced through them, muttering to herself as they climbed. A story seemed to be unfolding in curling white letters.

His gunshot missed me by a fraction of an inch. It tore the sleeve of my dress just a little. He came over to me, mortified at what he had done. 'I didn't mean to hit you,' he said. 'I couldn't believe my eyes when I saw you – in that green dress you are hidden against the leaves, like a piece of the forest itself.'

173

'That is exactly what I am,' I said . . .

The words trailed out, and Charity climbed a little higher.

> He said, 'Could I see you again? Perhaps I might come to your parents' house, or take you out to dinner on the other side of the woods?'
>
> 'I'm not sure,' I said, 'but first we might meet here from time to time, under the green leaves.'
>
> 'Really?' he said, looking puzzled.
>
> 'Yes, really,' I said, and smiled at him.
>
> 'You have a lovely smile,' he told me. 'What is your name?'

Charity stopped reading. The words had disappeared again, and now there was something else. Music. It was welling up through the chimney spaces around them. It was the waltz, that haunting little tune.

She turned to Silas. 'Do you hear that?' she said.

'Yes, I do. *Da dee da* . . .' He joined in with the tune.

'But where is it coming from?' Charity listened with her head cocked on one side.

'One of the rooms down there, by the sound of it.'

'Where are we, then?'

Silas shone the lantern through the chimney. 'I can see an empty grate; I'll go down and have a look.'

'I'll come with you,' Charity said straight away.

'I think you should stay up here. We're a long way from your room now. You don't want to get caught.'

'I don't care,' Charity said firmly. 'I'm coming too.'

The fireplace was in a box room piled high with tea chests and more. It was hard to make out a clear route between the boxes. With the help of the lantern they found their way to the door, which was unlocked. The corridor outside was empty, but Charity immediately recognized it as the green corridor in the west wing. They could hear the music again – the gentle lilting waltz echoing faintly from somewhere further up the corridor. On the opposite wall she saw the covered portrait.

'I want to show you something,' she whispered to Silas, beckoning for him to follow her. 'Hold the lantern steady.'

They crept over to the portrait. Charity took a deep breath and pulled the cloth away. 'There,' she said. 'There she is – that's my mother.' She looked up, smiling.

Only it wasn't her mother. It was a painting of a white unicorn, the same summer trees in the background, the same woodland setting. The creature even had a thin loop of green ribbon tied around its neck and its head was bowed down.

'I don't understand,' Charity said, confused.

'I saw her here. It was a painting of my mother, in this same frame, in this same place.'

'Are you sure?' Silas asked her. 'We could be in a corridor that looks similar to the other one.'

'No,' she insisted. 'It's the same one. Count the doors – one there – the nursery door – then another one, and then one more. Three in all. I just know it's this one.'

'Perhaps someone moved the painting or changed it over?' Silas suggested.

'But why would anyone do that?' Charity asked.

Silas shook his head. 'Why keep you shut away from everything and everybody like a prisoner? Nothing here makes sense. This is a weird house, and weird things seem to happen, especially to you. Mr Kawkins said that . . .' He trailed off into silence.

'What did he say?'

'Nothing. He didn't say nothing.'

'I think you meant to say he didn't say *anything*,

but I think he *did* say something, didn't he?"

'No,' Silas insisted.

'Come on, you can tell me. I thought we were friends . . .'

'We are,' Silas said. 'I don't want to upset you, that's all.'

'Why would it upset me?' Charity wondered.

'Because . . . because he said your mother was thought to be a witch.'

They were both silent for a moment. 'A witch,' Charity repeated quietly.

'Yes, they all thought so. She came from the forest, where the ancients are, and . . . and she did magic. That's true, isn't it? All that writing in the chimneys . . . that's magic, that is.'

'It *is* magic,' Charity agreed, 'but I don't think she was a witch. I think she was something else.'

She could barely think straight, and the strange whirling notes of music didn't help. All at once she saw an image of her mother clearly in her mind. She was writing in the fairy tale book and hiding it under the crib, directly under the hanging scissors. The music suddenly seemed to grow louder, as if it were calling out an urgent message among its spinning notes. She covered her ears.

'I'm sorry, Charity,' Silas said. 'I knew it would be upsetting, you see.'

'It's not you,' she told him. 'It's the music.'

Silas held his lamp higher and looked up and down the corridor. Then he turned back to Charity and his mouth fell open.

She took her hands from her ears and whispered, 'What?'

'You're all clean,' he said. 'No soot on you at all. Nothing.'

Charity looked down. Somehow she wasn't surprised. 'It happened before,' she said. 'I don't know why.'

'You're just like her,' he breathed, his eyes wide. 'Look at me, dirty all over, and not a mark on you.'

Charity nodded. 'I know, I know, but I don't know what it all means. I think I need to go and find the old lady – the midwife in the woods. She will know. How will I find her?'

'Easy. I'll take you,' Silas said. 'If I can get in and out, then so can you. I'll come and get you. We'll go tomorrow night.'

'Listen . . .' Charity murmured.

'What? I can't hear anything.'

'Exactly. The music has stopped.'

'So it has,' Silas said. The corridor was eerily quiet, apart from the creak and crack of the old floorboards under their feet. Charity tucked the dustsheet back over the painting, then they returned to the box room and climbed up through the chimney to Charity's bedroom.

'You'd better have some warm clothes ready tomorrow night,' Silas told her.

'I will,' she replied.

'Goodnight, then.'

'Goodnight, Silas, and thank you,' she said.

'You're welcome, miss.' And he vanished back up the chimney, only to pop back down a moment later. 'Sorry . . . Charity,' he said with a grin, and was gone.

Chapter Seventeen

Charity still had three squares of chocolate left from when Edward had put them under her pillow. Once Silas had left she hid them in the cupboard, along with the book of fairy tales. They might need some chocolate the following night.

In the morning, once she was dressed, she and Rose went down the back stairs. As she approached the kitchen door, Charity heard the friendly clink of cutlery on breakfast plates and low murmurs of conversation. She went in without knocking, and saw Edward, Mrs Browne and a strange man sitting at the table, finishing their breakfast. Not one of them noticed Charity as she stood in the shadow of the heavy curtain that hung from the back of the kitchen door to keep out the draughts.

'Good morning,' she said quietly.

The strange man, his mouth wide open, dropped his fork onto his plate with a loud clatter.

'My, my,' said Mrs Browne, smiling. 'Good morning, Miss Charity. You seem to have given one of us quite a fright, at least.'

'So that's her, is it?' the strange man asked the cook. Charity thought his words sounded a little slurred.

'This is Miss Delafield, yes, in as much as it concerns you,' Mrs Browne said with a curt nod at him and a smile for Charity.

'Been sleepwalking again, have you?' the man asked, wiping the back of his hand across his moustache and putting his china mug back on the table with thump. 'Only I've been employed to protect you from undesirables from the outside.'

He gestured vaguely in the direction of the forest. 'I've walked around the gardens all night, just to look after you,' he added with a smirk.

'If you've finished your breakfast, Mr Chambers, I suggest you get off now. It's been a long night for you,' Mrs Browne said pointedly.

Edward stood up, tall and broad in his black waistcoat and white shirt, and dabbed at his mouth with a napkin. 'I'll show you out,' he said firmly.

'No need. I can make my own way,' Mr Chambers said, standing up and bundling himself into his overcoat. He stood to attention, saluted Charity with a practised hand, then winked at her.

'Not Mister, you understand, but Sergeant Major Chambers. Retired, miss, in fact,' he said, balancing awkwardly, his hand held stiffly to his forehead. 'At your service.'

Charity could smell something harsh on his breath. He turned and bowed to the rest of the room, and Charity felt Rose's hand rest protectively on her shoulder.

'Good day to you all, and thank you for the breakfast, ma'am. I shall be back later to resume my night duties.'

After he had left, Mrs Browne said, 'I'm sorry you had to see that display, Miss Charity. After those footprints were found your father employed the sergeant major to patrol the fence at night. Seems to me he's been drinking from his hip flask a little too much. It's disgusting, that's what it is. Come on now – sit down and have your porridge.'

Charity took a seat at the table and Edward winked at her. 'Bit of a character, Sergeant Major Chambers,' he said.

'Not one we want to encourage,' Rose muttered.

Mr Tompkins slipped in through the door and Mrs Browne bent down to stroke him. 'Now there's my fine cat. Come on, you dear old puss, come and see what Mrs Browne has for you.' The cat rubbed round her legs as she fetched some trimmings from the meat safe.

'You spoil that cat, Mrs Browne,' Edward said, smiling.

'He's a special cat, aren't you?' Mrs Browne ruffled his ears.

'He's a witch's cat,' Charity said quietly.

Suddenly everyone was silent. The only noise came from a log shifting in the big fireplace. Mrs Browne paused in her stroking, looked up and said, 'Now what makes you say that, Miss Charity?'

Charity blushed. 'Well, he's black all over with those green eyes. He's like a cat in a fairy tale.'

'That old woman at the gate the other morning . . . did she say anything to you? Anything about Mr Tompkins?'

'No,' Charity said. 'She said she remembered him as a kitten, that was all.'

'So she *did* speak to you,' Rose said, looking around at the others with concern across her face. For a moment there was an expectant hush. It was as if they were all about to speak but no one wanted to be first. Edward cleared his throat, but it was Mrs Browne who finally broke the silence.

'Well, you're not an old witch's cat, are you?' she said to Mr Tompkins.

'Finish your porridge,' Rose told Charity. 'Then a short walk outside, and after that it's time for lessons.'

The snow was almost entirely gone now, but it was still cold enough for Charity to wear her long red coat.

They kept to the top path so that she could see little beyond the railings but a smudge of winter trees. She looked up at the roof and the tall chimneys. Would she really be climbing along there later? They passed below the forbidden wing, dark and closed off with its four blank windows looking down on the garden pathways like two pairs of dead eyes; open but with nothing behind them.

Charity spent the afternoon on another set of horrible maths problems about how fast two carriages were going as they passed each other, and how many buckets of water it would take to fill a cistern. She could see the gloomy cistern clearly in her head: it was a great square lead-lined hole somewhere out in the forest. She could also see the poor peasant, looking like a scarecrow in his rags, filling it so slowly, tipping in bucket after bucket of water and counting . . . all the time counting. When she looked up from her page, it was already dark.

Rose came in and took Charity's exercise books away for marking. 'Mrs Browne has made a good warming stew, but now she is busy in the kitchen, preparing something for the church. She wonders if you would mind eating later tonight, in the nursery?'

After she had eaten, Charity sat at the nursery table, warmed by a cosy fire. She pictured the network of chimneys above the fireplace going all over the house, linking the rooms. She saw her mother's writing in the soot, stretching out above and around her. She needed to know more; she needed to know what had happened to her mother, and what her connection to the ancients was.

She went to the window and looked out into the garden. Sergeant Major Chambers was marching along beside the railings carrying a lantern, stopping every now and then to shine it around before moving on. She and Silas would have to be careful, she thought.

Wandering away from the window, Charity idly set her old rocking horse moving. She pushed its head so that it rocked gently to and fro. As she did so, she felt something on its forehead that she had never noticed before. Puzzled, she pulled the red leather brow band away from the carved section of mane that tumbled down between its ears. There was a neat lump there, in a perfect circle. She rubbed it with her fingers, then studied it carefully.

Thinking hard, she went straight back to her bedroom, then knelt down and rummaged in the cupboard where her shoes were kept. Her hand closed on the little twist of wood that she had assumed was one of Mrs Browne's seaside souvenirs. She looked closely at it. There were traces of white paint, and the twist certainly came to a point.

Her heart was racing now. Was this the horn the old lady had told her to find?

She took it back to the nursery and approached the rocking horse slowly, almost fearfully. She didn't want to be wrong. She brought the little piece of wood out from behind her back as if she were surprising the horse with the gift. She pulled the red brow band aside and held the twist of wood against the bump on its forehead.

Her rocking horse had not been a horse at all.

She had always loved it. She had played on it for hours when she was much younger. Now she looked at it and saw it very differently. She was sure of it now: it had once been a unicorn, just like the one painted above the door in the closed-off nursery, just like the one in the storybook, just like the one in the old spinning top.

She climbed up onto the unicorn, still holding the little twisted horn against its forehead, and sat in the saddle. She closed her eyes and rocked slowly back and forth. She remembered the feeling very well – the sensation of galloping forward, of being part of a continuous and wonderful story, of playing and imagining things and wondering about magic. She had been much younger, of course. When had that stopped? Almost all her life she had been discouraged from such play by a series of nannies and tutors, who blended into one in her mind before the arrival of kindly Rose. And her father had taken away her mythology books and fairy stories. Why else should she feel the need to hide the book that she had found under the little crib?

She let the rocking unicorn slow to a halt and

sat on it for a moment or two longer in the evening stillness. Soon it would be time for bed. Time to wait for Silas.

After her hair was brushed, after she had washed and cleaned her teeth, after she had said her prayers and Mr Tompkins had been shooed out into the corridor, she was finally left alone in bed.

The key clicked in the lock.

She opened the book of fairy stories, but she couldn't concentrate. She knew she had to stay awake, but her thoughts were so muddled that she finally drifted off into sleep, and the book fell out of her hands.

In her dream, Charity looked around at the dim shapes of the paintings and the draped marble busts in the corridor. She could just see the glassy-eyed stare of the stuffed animal heads. It was cold and very dark, and everything looked so stark and haunted and unwelcoming. There were so many oddly-shaped lumps, and so many dark, shadowy areas too, where anything could be hidden and waiting.

'Come on,' she whispered to Mr Tompkins. She moved away from the door towards the uncarpeted stairs that led to the kitchen. The cat was blocking her way, as if he didn't want her to go down there, and she nearly tripped over him. 'Silly old puss,' she said, lifting him aside.

Edward's voice came out of the darkness: 'Now, now, Miss Charity. Whatever are you doing out of bed? You are either sleepwalking, or dreaming, or both. Miss Rose and I will take you straight back to your room.'

Suddenly a powerful man's voice rang out, and everything went quiet. 'You should get back to bed at once, my dear. There is nothing to see here,' the voice said. A door opened in the darkness, and Sergeant Major Chambers came in with a tall, pale man, who would have been considered handsome were it not for the sad expression on his face. It was Charity's father, but he looked much younger. Between them they were carrying something very big, wrapped up in a cloth such as the sweep had spread out before he began his work.

Charity stepped slowly into the pool of light cast by the open door. Inside the room, candles were set out on the table in long lines, and there were scattered lamps too. It was a big room – big enough to be a ballroom. Music was playing somewhere in the distance – the waltz tune.

'I understand that you rode on your horse today,' the young man who was Charity's father said.

She found herself looking down at her bare feet, and nodding very slightly.

'I should remind you that such rides are a privilege, and not a right. It seems to me that you have picked up some sort of fever, because you have apparently been seeing unusual things too.'

Her father placed the flat of his cold palm

against Charity's forehead. 'You certainly feel hot. Straight to bed with you at once – and be thankful I haven't given you some cleansing physic. I heard you creaking on the rockers of that toy, but Sergeant Major Chambers and I have something nicer for you to ride – something that will make you feel much better. Be patient – it is all wrapped up here. I have been hunting this creature for a long, long time – look.'

Edward stepped out into the light and helped Sergeant Major Chambers and her father to steady whatever was wrapped up in the big cloth. Charity felt Mr Tompkins at her feet, felt him shrink back in agitation against her legs as the cloth was suddenly pulled off—

'Charity!' an urgent voice called out, waking her. She stirred and half clung to the remnant of the dream as the sweep's cloth fell to the ground. Something beautiful – something magical – had been about to appear.

She opened her eyes. Silas was standing by the bed.

'Come on,' he said. 'No time to waste. The old man is round the other side of the house; we haven't got long.'

Charity got out of bed slowly, still dazed by her dream. She stuffed her feet into a pair of soft leather boots and pulled her red coat on over her nightdress. She dug out the chocolate too and put it in her pocket. Silas was already up the chimney; she could see the light spilling down from his lantern. He hauled her up after him.

'Look,' he said, and lifted up his lamp to shine across the walls of the chimney. 'All gone.'

It was true. Her mother's words had vanished. The insides of the chimney showed only the solid, soft, even black of undisturbed soot.

'I think I must have read what I needed to read,' Charity said.

They climbed up the wide flue and then followed an angled tunnel to the big chimney itself. Silas went up first and sat on the edge. Charity inched her way up the space with her back against one side and her feet extended against the opposite wall, until she was near enough for Silas to lift her up. He had turned off his lamp, and they sat in the dark on top of the very highest chimney, with just the moon and pinpoints of starlight overhead.

'Look,' Silas whispered, and he pointed down to the railings on the far side of the park, where a lantern was slowly moving. 'That's where he is now. We have to climb down and beat him to that side. He's slow but steady – well, he is this early on . . . Once he's emptied his hip flask he slows down.'

Silas climbed off the top of the chimney onto the stone surround and helped Charity down. It was narrow and she could see, even in the dim light, that it was crumbling in places. She held onto Silas in fear as they made their way round the side of the chimney. There was a narrow strip of lead flashing, just wide enough to allow them to walk carefully along the top of the roof in single file. At the other end, Silas pointed out the wide black drainpipe lip. 'We climb down from there,' he said.

The corner bricks were laid in such a way that they could be used as very shallow steps, and they climbed slowly down to the path, clutching the drainpipe as they went. They ran across to the railings, dodging the looming statues and the clipped trees. Silas hoisted himself up the railings, pulled an old sack out of his bag, and laid it over the spikes. He reached down and helped Charity up, then dropped onto the road beyond.

Charity heard his boots land with a *thump*. She realized that this was the furthest she had ever been from the house. In the moment before she allowed herself to drop down outside for the first time ever, away from safety and the only world she knew, she paused and closed her eyes and listened to the night. There was a breeze stirring the trees, and it whistled through her hair too. It was cold, but it did not make her shiver; she welcomed the feel of it. An owl hooted somewhere among the trees, and she was sure she could hear little things scurrying along the forest floor.

Silas called up to her softly. 'Come on! Don't be scared. Jump down – I'll catch you.'

'I'm not scared,' Charity said. 'I'm not scared of anything at all.'

She felt a surge of strange energy, a certainty that what she was doing was right, and jumped down from the railings.

'We need to go this way,' she said, pointing to a narrow gap between two beech trees. She wasn't sure how she knew the way, but something told her that this was where the path lay.

'All right,' said Silas, but Charity had already set off. He would have to run after her now, just to keep up.

Chapter Eighteen

As soon as Charity stepped between the trees she felt different again – as if she were alive for the first time; as if some special switch or tap had been turned on inside her. She was suddenly very aware of the forest around her. She could smell the cold mulch on the ground, still wet from snow melt, together with last season's leaves and the fungal smell of the damp things leeching onto the tree roots. She could smell animals, each with its own distinct warm scent, and she knew them all: foxes and badgers, and even the smaller things hiding deep in the ground; their lairs lay deep in amongst the trees, their stores of food buried for the winter.

Charity knew where she had to go too; which path to take through the trees. Silas trotted along beside her, aware of a change in his friend, a sudden burst of confidence. He tried to get in front of her, and waved his lamp hopefully at the trees ahead to light the way.

'That's very kind,' she said, 'but I know exactly where we have to be, and I won't need the lamp to get us there.'

Eventually they came to a little house tucked away amongst a grove of dark trees. A golden light was burning in the window and a plume of white wood smoke drifted up from a little iron chimney on the roof. The house was oddly shaped and looked as if it had grown naturally out of the surrounding trees, which were clearly ancient, with enormous trunks, gnarled, twisted roots and low-hanging branches. It was as if the trees had reached a certain height and then curved back down to the ground again, sprouting smaller trees where they had touched the earth.

'This is the old yew grove . . .' Silas said, looking around wide-eyed and speaking very quietly, as if the trees might somehow be disturbed by his voice. 'Old Kawkins told me about it. It's very old, he said. It's been here for hundreds – even thousands of years.'

'I know,' Charity said, and walked up to the little house, ducking under the low, curving branches. She knocked on the front door.

There was a brief moment when all they could hear was the wind sighing loudly through the trees. Then the door opened, and the old lady was standing on the porch.

'So you've come at last, my dear,' she said, smiling at Charity.

'Yes, with the help of my friend Silas,' Charity told her. Silas nodded nervously.

'Come in, both of you.'

Inside, the little house was clean and warm

and smelled of green things – of wet herbs and leaves. Charity realized that she could identify them all. Her mind raced to name each one: feverfew and borage and lavender and wormwood and eye-bright.

There was a fire burning in the grate, and two battered-looking old armchairs were pulled up close to it.

'Sit there, my dears, and warm yourselves,' said the old lady.

She eased herself into one of the chairs while Charity and Silas squeezed into the other.

'You got my letter, then?' she said.

'No' – Charity shook her head – 'I didn't see any letter.'

The woman nodded. 'I put one through the railings for you. No matter – you are here now, and that's all that matters. Why, you don't even know my name, do you? I know that you are Miss Charity Delafield of Stone Green Hall, and that this friend of yours is old Kawkins's boy.'

'His name is Silas Jones,' Charity said.

'Welcome, Charity, and welcome, Silas. My name is Mrs Elkins, but please call me Sarah. Look . . .' And she held up the gold foil wrapping from the chocolate that Charity had given her at the gate.

'You gave me a gift,' she said. 'You are a good and kind child.'

'I have more,' said Charity, pulling out the three squares of chocolate and unwrapping them.

Sarah took a square but wrapped it up in the gold foil again. 'For later,' she said. 'Now, let me look at you properly, my dear.'

Charity gave the second square of chocolate to Silas, then popped the last one into her mouth while Sarah gazed at her. She savoured the sweetness of it on her tongue.

'Your hair glows in the firelight, just as hers used to . . .' Sarah sighed. 'You are her child, all right. You are the half-faerie girl we lost.'

Charity swallowed the chocolate quickly, her eyes wide. 'Half faerie?' she repeated.

Sarah nodded. 'Yes. You found my house on your own, didn't you, my dear child? All the way through the trees to the deep part of the forest? You did not need Silas here to show you after he helped you out of the big house. You knew exactly where to come, didn't you?'

'Well . . . yes, I did,' Charity was still trying to understand what everything meant.

'You knew with a certainty. And I think you know other things for certain too, don't you?'

'Yes,' Charity whispered, feeling almost pinned to the chair by Sarah's gaze. The old lady no longer appeared frail or vulnerable, as she had that day at the gate. She seemed strong now; a little fierce – but kind.

'Tell me about my mother,' Charity said. 'My father never talks of her. It's almost as if she never existed. I know he loved her, though, because he has a hidden portrait of her, and he

went and looked at it on her birthday. I saw it –
she was very beautiful.'

'Oh, yes, your mother was beautiful, my child,
but it must be said that she was wild and wilful
too. She was beautiful as the sky or a river is
beautiful, or as a wild animal is beautiful. She was
a force of nature, and your father loved her.'

Sarah's face seemed to darken at the mention
of Charity's father. She leaned forward in her
chair. 'He loved her, but he took her away from
us.'

'Us . . . ?' Charity asked.

Sarah's face brightened suddenly. 'Where are
my manners?' she cried. 'It's a cold night and I
haven't even offered you poor children a drink.
I shall make you something good and warming.'

She went through a low door into the kitchen
at the back of the house.

'I think we should go now, while we can,' Silas
said quietly. 'I don't like it here. She's a witch, and
she's going to give us a potion – I just know it.'

'I need to find out more,' Charity whispered. 'I don't know what she meant about being half faerie. I can't go now.'

'I think it's dangerous here,' Silas muttered.

'I feel I'm in danger at home, but not here,' Charity told him. 'I want to know more, and she's the only person I can ask.'

'Don't drink what she gives us, though. Promise.'

Charity shook her head at her friend. 'I can't promise that.'

'Here we are, my children.' Sarah came back in with two cups. One was white with roses painted on it, and the other was a deep green colour with a roundel showing a picture of a house.

'I've seen that cup before,' Charity realized as Sarah passed it to her.

'Well, I should hope so,' the old lady said. 'It is part of your mother's wedding china. A whole service was made for her and your father as a present on their wedding day. She gave me this cup, and the matching saucer.'

Silas took his cup and put it on the table. He folded his arms. Charity sniffed the steam coming from her cup and took a small sip. It was tea sweetened with honey, a special honey. Her senses raced to identify it. Acacia blossom honey. Somehow she just knew that this is what it was.

'That's right,' Sarah said. 'Honey from my own beehives here in the grove. Sweet like bottled summer.'

Charity stared. 'How did you know what I was . . .?'

'What you were thinking, my dear? I know lots of things. I know that your friend here won't drink his tea because he thinks I am a witch, and that it must be a potion which will put him under a spell.' She wiggled her fingers in the air and rolled her eyes at Silas. 'Some people call me a witch, I know they do. Not to my face, but behind my poor old stooped back. I'm sure your father is one of them, Charity. He would be very angry if he knew you were here with me.'

Charity took a deep breath. Now was the time to ask what she wanted to know. 'What really happened to my mother?'

'Well, she did not die giving birth to you. I know, because I was there.'

'So how did she die?' Charity peered nervously over the edge of the teacup.

'The simple answer is that she didn't die. But I think that in your heart you were already as certain of that as you were of finding the way to my house tonight.'

'Yes,' Charity said, allowing herself to smile. 'I was sure of it. I knew that somehow she was calling to me.'

'You are right, my child. She has been calling to you all these years. You had the dreams, didn't you?'

Charity nodded. 'And I found her diary –

except the words floated off the page and up into the chimneys.'

'Yes, I am sure. She protected the words with a spell, you see, so that only you could read them. She was telling you about herself; she was showing you the truth. You see, my child, your mother is one of the ancients – one of the faerie. They have lived in this forest for hundreds of years. And, like me, you are one half faerie and one half mortal. Now you must answer your poor mother's call. When you gave me that kind gift the morning we met at the gate, I knew you had the heart to do it. Your poor mother is lost, you see, and only you can find her and set her free.'

'How?' Charity asked.

Sarah gazed at her. 'I wonder if you finally found that precious horn I told you about . . . that little piece of twisted wood – that scrap, which looked like nothing more than a piece of driftwood?'

Charity nodded. 'I did.'

'Then you must know by now that it fits onto your toy unicorn, which was made for you by one of the ancients here in the grove. He carved it out of old and sacred yew wood. My child, I must tell you about the horn—'

Suddenly a dazzling bright light flashed in at the window, and they heard voices. The door was flung open and Charity's father, Mr Kawkins and Sergeant Major Chambers crowded into the doorway.

Silas stood up and the colour drained from his face.

'What did I tell you, sir?' Mr Kawkins cried. 'He's been sneaking out most evenings – on some fools' errand with your girl here. Did you think I hadn't noticed, boy?'

Mr Delafield said, 'Charity, come here at once and stand beside me.'

'But Father—'

'There will be no buts and no arguments of

any kind. You will do as I say, this instant. And do not try to pretend, as you have been doing, that this is an example of your so-called somnambulism. You have made your way here wilfully and wide awake, no doubt encouraged by this lady. Your letter was found, madam, so do not try to deny that you have tried to contact my daughter.'

'Good evening, gentlemen,' Sarah said quietly, a sweet expression on her face. 'Good evening, Charles. I have indeed encouraged your daughter to visit me, so that she may learn the truth about herself. May I offer you some tea, perhaps? I do not wish to appear inhospitable, and it is a cold night.'

'You, madam, have been filling my daughter's head with arrant nonsense. Of that I have no doubt.'

Charity stood up defiantly and faced her father. 'This lady has told me something that I already knew in my heart. She has told me that my mother is not dead after all.'

'It is far worse than I feared . . .' he muttered. 'Chambers, take hold of her.'

Then he turned his attention to the old woman, who sat perfectly still and upright in her armchair. 'You have been waiting for your chance to corrupt my child. Well, much good may it do you. She will be going far away tomorrow, to an institution where she will be safe from all your dangerous and damaging piffle.'

Charity stared at her father open-mouthed. 'Tomorrow?' she asked weakly.

The old woman met his gaze without flinching. 'Charles,' she said, 'it is not "piffle", as you call it. Ariella lives.'

Mr Delafield's whole body was shaking with anger, but his voice was quiet. 'There is no hope of that. It has been twelve years, with no sign. The case has been closed – no one will look for her any longer. Even if they did, we both know that there is no chance of her being found.'

The old woman shook her head. 'I had a message,' she said softly. 'What I say is the truth.'

Mr Kawkins had been following the exchange, turning his head from side to side as they spoke. Now he reached out and roughly pulled Silas towards him. 'I'll take him back with me now, sir, if I may. The hour is late.'

Mr Delafield turned. 'Of course – go at once. This is all nonsense anyway, and we are leaving. Chambers, keep hold of my daughter.'

The sergeant major winked at Charity while pinning her arms close to her side.

Mr Delafield handed Mr Kawkins a gold coin from his pocket. 'Thank you,' he said. 'I am obliged for your help.'

'I am the one who should be obliged,' Mr Kawkins said. 'Goodnight to you, sir.'

'It's true!' Silas suddenly called out. 'We saw magic things. There was writing in the soot all over the chimney walls – messages from Charity's mother. I saw them!'

'Come on, lad,' Mr Kawkins said. 'This old woman's befuddled you with her witch's potion.'

'I'll find you,' Silas called out to Charity as he was dragged from the house. 'I'll find you, I promise.'

'I know you will,' she called back to him, struggling to break free of Sergeant Major Chambers. 'Father, please listen!'

'I hold the hunting rights over this forest,' Mr Delafield said, fixing Sarah with his gaze. 'If I find you trying to contact my daughter again, I will have this piece of land stripped and cleared for health reasons.'

'You couldn't,' the old woman told him.

'I wonder if you are willing to risk finding out?' he asked. 'Sergeant Major Chambers, please take my daughter outside.'

Charity was dragged out of the cottage, her heels scraping against the floor as she went. Through the window she could see her father talking to Sarah. His face was red now, and he repeatedly punched the palm of his hand with his fist.

The night air and night smells crowded in around Charity again. She saw that the path through the trees was lit up, as if by a ghostly, greenish light like phosphorescence – a path back to the road and home.

A shout from Mr Delafield distracted Sergeant Major Chambers, and for just a moment Charity felt his grip on her arms loosen. It was enough for her to break free and run down the path and away from him. She was immediately swallowed up by darkness. She heard shouts behind her, but she quickly weaved her way through the trees, and the pursuing voices were soon lost. Suddenly she saw a dark shape running towards her. It was Silas.

'I ran off to help you,' he said, his breath misting in the cold night air, 'and here you are.'

'They're following us. Come on,' Charity gasped. 'We haven't much time.' She stretched out her hand, and Silas grabbed it and hung on as they ran.

Charity felt that strange surge of certainty again – along with an astonishing sense of speed and power. She pulled Silas's slight figure after her, almost lifting him off his feet as they ran. Everything in the dark forest was as clear as day to her. A wide-eyed deer fled beside them – until they reached the edge of the forest and the house was in sight. Then it lowered its head and allowed Charity to stroke its trembling neck for a moment, before bounding off, zigzagging back into the trees.

Chapter Nineteen

Mr Delafield's voice came echoing through the forest, shouting Charity's name. There were other voices too, and they were close now. She pulled Silas across the road to where the sack still lay over the top of the railings. They climbed up and dropped down into the gardens. Mr Tompkins came running up to them, and Charity picked him up and hugged him.

'Oh, Mr Tompkins,' she said, burying her face in his warm fur.

He struggled in her arms and then dropped down to the ground. Turning to look up at her briefly, he dashed off towards the west wing.

Charity followed him. 'Come on,' she said, and Silas hurried along behind her, his boots clattering on the path.

When they reached the overgrown wall, Mr Tompkins launched himself up and began to climb the twisted stems and branches. Charity looked up at the row of four high, blank windows . . . except that now she suddenly noticed that one of them was not so blank. A silvery light seemed to be flowing out of the furthest window, swirling around the blank face of the glass and sparkling slightly like frost. Charity looked at the other three windows, which were as dark as ever . . . and something clicked into place in her head – the odd problem that had been slowly unravelling there. If a corridor has three doors but there are four windows visible on the outside, what does that mean?

'It means,' she said out loud, 'that one of the doors has been blocked up. There is another room on that corridor, a hidden room. That is where Mr Tompkins is going.'

'What's that?' Silas said, aware of a noise from beyond the railings. 'We must get into the house. Come on.'

Charity saw that the kitchen lights were still on. She grabbed Silas's hand, and they dashed up the avenue of statues. They burst straight into the kitchen, still holding hands. Edward, Rose and Mrs Browne were all sitting at the table, sipping hot tea.

Edward stood up. 'Whatever is going on, Miss Charity? Are you all right?'

'My dear child,' Rose said, coming over to her. 'Where on earth have you been?'

'Never mind any of that now,' Charity said firmly. 'We must hide Silas. My father will be here any minute, and he will certainly lock me in my room, and he is sending me away tomorrow – but it won't matter because Silas can help me out later and it was never more important – please!'

Rose and Edward stared at her in astonishment, but Mrs Browne stood up. 'Come with me, young man – quickly now,' she said. 'I know a place.'

'What on earth are you doing, Mrs Browne?' asked Rose.

'What we must all do . . .' Mrs Browne told her.

She took Silas off through the scullery. Rose and Edward stood together awkwardly. Charity looked at the two of them and saw a flaring golden light playing about them, as if they had their backs to the sun.

'You two must marry,' she said, smiling. 'I know it. I see you together. I see the love – I see it so clearly.'

'Miss Charity,' Rose said, looking pink and flustered, 'has something happened to you? Are you unwell?'

'I am well and I am strong,' she replied.

The door was flung open with a bang that

brought a gust of cold air into the room and set the candles and lamps fluttering. Charity's father and Sergeant Major Chambers came stamping in.

'Thank heavens,' Mr Delafield said. 'I see that you have at least had the sense to come home, Charity. Where has that sweep's boy got to? Did he come in here with you?'

'No,' Charity said defiantly. 'Of course not. He was terrified by everything that happened and ran home to wait for Mr Kawkins and be punished. I came in here by myself.'

'Is this true?' Mr Delafield asked Rose.

There was a pause; a flicker of hesitation. Rose looked directly at Charity, and then, after a brief glance at Edward, replied, 'She came running in all on her own.'

Charity's heart lifted.

Mrs Browne bustled in from the scullery, wiping her hands on a tea towel. 'Good evening, sir,' she said. 'Glad to see you managed to bring her back safe, poor mite.'

'Yes,' he replied. 'She is a poor deluded child. Perhaps a warm drink for her, Mrs Browne, after all that running about in the cold night air? I don't want her to catch a chill.'

'Of course, sir. The kettle is always hot.' Mrs Browne went to the cupboard and fetched down her tin of cocoa powder. 'I think just this once . . . don't you, sir?'

'Yes, by all means.' Mr Delafield nodded and then turned to Rose. 'She must be taken to her room immediately, I'm afraid, and locked in, and I must insist that you spend the rest of the night with her, making sure that she stays there. Her head has been filled with fantastical nonsense by that old woman – the old village midwife. I believe I showed you the letter addressed to my daughter that she threw over the railings – the one that Sergeant Major Chambers found earlier?'

Chambers gave a little salute at the mention of his name.

223

'That's right, you did, sir,' said Rose.

Mrs Browne passed the cup of hot chocolate to Mr Delafield. His hand moved briefly over the cup, through the rising steam, then he gave it to Charity. It smelled wonderful. He watched her drink. 'That's the way,' he said. 'Drink it all up now – it'll make you feel better.'

She drained the cup and put it back on the table. Suddenly her father pulled her close and held her in his arms. Such a thing had never happened before – as far back as she could remember.

'My poor child,' he said, and when she looked up at him, she saw that his eyes were wet. 'So like your mother, so sadly afflicted . . .' He let go of her at once, and almost pushed her away.

Rose came over and gently took Charity by the shoulders. 'Come on – time for bed.'

'Now,' Mr Delafield said, 'Sergeant Major Chambers here will resume his patrol of the park, and my sincere apologies to you all for the interruption to your evening. An apology, if you please, from you, Charity, for being the cause of so much worry and disruption.'

'Goodnight, everyone, and I am sorry for running off like that. It won't happen again,' Charity said very quietly.

Rose took her by the hand; Edward followed with a lamp, and they led her up the stairs. Charity glanced back and saw her father staring after them, a look of anguish on his face.

Once they were out of her father's sight, Charity stopped suddenly and said, 'I'm not deluded, Rose, I promise. And thank you for not giving Silas away.'

'I don't know what came over me just now, lying like that to Mr Delafield,' Rose whispered. 'I must have taken leave of my senses.' She smoothed down her long skirt nervously.

'Maybe you've just come to them . . . your senses, I mean,' Edward said. 'I really don't see what harm it could do for Charity to visit an old lady who is probably just as lonely as she is.'

'That's quite enough of that. It was very late and very dark and very cold, and she was out in that wild, dangerous forest, of all places. Why, any parent would be worried.'

'Only if you're scared of rabbits,' Edward muttered.

'Come now, Edward,' Rose said sharply. 'There's more than rabbits over there, and you should know that. I don't want to get into trouble.'

'What is the worst trouble that you could get into?' Charity asked.

'Why, Miss Charity, I could lose my job for a start.'

'Well, you will be marrying Edward soon enough. He can look after you.'

Rose flushed. 'That's quite enough of that. Whatever has possessed you to say such things? I don't know what's got into you today, Miss Charity, I really don't.'

'Yes you do, Rose,' Edward said. 'This innocent child has seen the truth over the weeks and months, and to her it's simple. She has seen that there is a feeling, that there is even love between us. I know that you are scared of it, and up till now, here, tonight, I have been scared too.' He got down on one knee in the narrow corridor that led to Charity's room. 'But I'm not scared any more. Will you marry me, Rose Constance Marwick?'

'Say yes, Rose!' Charity said. 'Go on – you *must*!'

'You've both gone mad,' Rose said, her cheeks pink. 'Now get up. Supposing someone found you fooling around like that?'

'I wouldn't care,' Edward told her. As he straightened up, the lamp threw his broad shadow across the ceiling. 'And do you know what? I would tell them so as well.'

'I think the whole world's gone mad tonight. What on earth has got into you both? Has everyone been put under some sort of spell?' Rose asked.

'Yes,' Edward said. 'I am under *your* spell, Rose, and I have been since you came here.'

'Enough,' she said and, flustered, took her key-ring out of her pocket. Charity spotted the green ribbon with the key to the west wing on it. Even if Silas couldn't reach her, at least she knew where the key was.

Rose opened Charity's door. 'Come on now. Into bed with you.'

Chapter Twenty

Rose made Edward stay in the room with Charity while she went to change into her own nightdress.

'Thank you for the chocolate, Edward,' Charity said, sitting up in her bed. 'I gave another piece to the old lady in the forest and she saved it for later.'

'I don't suppose she has much of that sort of thing, does she?' Edward said. 'Poor old soul. When I was young we used to dare ourselves to go near her house. We all thought she was a witch.'

'She's not a witch. She's the same as me.'

'Oh,' said Edward. 'And what's that, then?'

'I'm half faerie,' Charity said proudly.

'What's all this?' Rose bustled in wearing her dressing gown. 'What are you two talking about?'

'I was telling Edward – I'm half faerie,' Charity told her.

'You really have had your head filled with nonsense, haven't you?'

'I wouldn't be so sure, Rose,' Edward said. 'I grew up around here, and people talked about such things.'

Rose sighed. 'Don't you go and make it worse. Off with you now. It's late, and Miss here needs to sleep off whatever spell it is she's under.'

'Goodnight, Edward,' Charity said.

'Goodnight, Miss Charity, Miss Rose. Do I get a goodnight kiss, then?' he added, turning to Rose.

'No, you certainly don't!' She opened the door to allow him out.

'I'll go, then,' he said.

'I think that would be best.'

Rose gave Edward the key to the bedroom door. 'Lock this door after you, please.'

'Supposing Miss Charity needs the bath-room?' Edward said, clearly playing for time.

'Then she may use the chamber pot, as she usually does,' Rose replied. She closed the door firmly, and she and Charity listened for the sharp click of the key.

'There,' said Rose. 'Now, if you wouldn't mind settling down . . . I don't think I can stand any more alarm or excitements tonight.'

'Where will you sleep?' Charity said from her own narrow little bed.

Rose took some blankets and a spare pillow down from the cupboard, and spread them out on the floor in front of the door.

'Here will suit me,' she said, leaning over to turn off the lamp.

'I want to read one of my stories,' Charity

said. 'Please, could you leave it on for a moment?'

'I'm sorry, I cannot allow that tonight. It's late and you really must get some sleep – and, for that matter, so must I.' With that, Rose extinguished the lamp and the room was plunged in darkness.

Charity lay there quietly. She kept her head still on the pillows even though it was bursting with excitement at everything she had discovered. She now knew that there was a closed-off room at the end of the corridor in the west wing. Four windows and three doors – now it made sense. Someone had sealed up the room – her father, perhaps? That must be where the music was coming from.

She lay awake for a very long time, expecting Silas to appear and take her to the hidden room. She heard the clocks chiming out the hours. But there was no sign of Silas, and she drifted into a deep sleep.

She opened her eyes and sat up at once. The

room was full of sunlight, the curtains were pulled back, and Rose was up and dressed and quietly putting some of Charity's clothes into a trunk.

Charity almost fell out of bed.

'My,' said Rose. 'Awake at last. You really needed that sleep.'

'What time is it?' Charity asked.

'Time for you to go and wash, and then come back here and have your hair brushed. We must hurry. I am afraid that the carriage will be here to take you to the school directly after breakfast – your father is determined.' Rose's voice broke a little as she spoke, but she quickly controlled herself.

Charity felt as if she couldn't breathe. Carriage? School? How could it be morning? Where was Silas? Where had he got to last night when she had needed him, and why had she slept so long? She had a vision of her father's hand passing across her cup of hot chocolate the

233

night before. He had given her something . . . a sleeping pill, a sedative.

'Rose,' she said. 'Did my father put something in my drink last night to make me sleep?'

'I very much doubt that. Now come along – bathroom, please.'

When Charity returned to her room, she put on her grey wool dress with the cotton pinafore. There was no other choice – all her clothes had been packed and the trunk was locked shut. Rose was standing by the dressing table with the brush.

'Good girl. Now just sit here, please.'

Charity stared at her pale face in the looking glass. She would not go to that school this morning. She was determined.

Rose pulled the brush through her hair. It caught in the tangles and it hurt, but Charity would not let it show. She sat up straight, and allowed the brush to tug down, snagging and catching at every stroke.

'You *are* being good this morning,' Rose commented.

'Please don't let him send me away,' Charity said quietly. 'I need to stay here. I have found out something about my mother.'

'Now, don't start that again,' Rose said. 'None of us want to see you sent off to that school, but you won't help yourself by coming out with all this fanciful nonsense.'

'It's not fanciful at all,' Charity insisted. 'My mother has been sending me messages through those fairy stories, and she wrote things from her diary in the soot in the chimneys: my father found her in the forest when he tried to hunt a unicorn, and he injured her by accident, but they fell in love anyway, and my rocking horse was once a unicorn but somehow it lost its horn – I can show it to you.'

Rose stopped brushing. 'You see, miss, you should listen to yourself. None of that made any sense. These imaginings are part of your sad condition, I think.'

'You make it sound as if I'm mad,' Charity said.

Rose did not reply – just carried on brushing Charity's hair.

'I'm not mad, Rose.'

'I certainly hope that is true.'

Charity stood up and went over to the cupboard where her old shoes were still piled up.

'I haven't finished your hair yet,' Rose protested.

'I just have to show you something. I found this in the scullery.' Charity pulled out the little twisted point of white wood and handed it to Rose.

'It's just a dirty old piece of wood,' she said. 'It might carry a disease. We ought to throw it on the fire at once.'

'No!' Charity snatched it back. 'It fits. It's the horn from the toy unicorn. At least let me show you.'

'It's time to go and have breakfast with your

father,' Rose told her. 'I'm sorry, but there is no time for any of this. Your father tells me that you will have a long journey to the institution.'

'It won't take a minute to show you what I mean,' Charity pleaded.

Rose hesitated and looked at her pocket watch. 'Very well, then,' she said. 'But we must be quick.'

Once they were in the nursery Charity pulled aside the brow band on her rocking horse.

'There,' she said. 'Look.' She held the twisted piece of wood against the raised circular nub. 'It fits perfectly.'

'So it does,' Rose agreed, 'but that doesn't mean anything. It only proves that it was once part of this old toy. Perhaps it was thought to be dangerous? A sharp point sticking out like that might injure a small child.'

'No. You don't understand – it's a unicorn, and that means something,' Charity told her.

'You have the key on the green ribbon, Rose. Let's go at once to the west wing and I'll show you where the secret room is.'

Rose took her firmly by the hand. 'Stop this. It's time to go down to breakfast. I should throw that dirty old thing away if I were you.'

Charity wrenched her hand free and tucked the wooden horn into her pinafore pocket. 'I will never throw it away,' she cried. 'It's important. I know it is.'

Rose sighed. 'Well, at least don't let your father see it.' She shut the nursery door and they walked along the corridor to the staircase.

Charity stopped suddenly. 'Wait,' she said. 'I haven't seen Mr Tompkins this morning.'

'I haven't seen him either,' Rose told her.

'The last time I saw him he was climbing up the wall of the west wing. He might be trapped in the hidden room!'

'I very much doubt that,' Rose said sharply. 'Hidden room, indeed. He's probably rubbing around Mrs Browne's legs in the kitchen, looking for a treat as usual. Now, come on. The clock is ticking.'

'I won't be going,' Charity said.

'Please don't cause any trouble this morning.' Rose sounded weary. 'I have no doubt you will be back for the holidays. There will be other girls of your own age too. It won't be so bad – you'll see.'

Charity said nothing.

Chapter Twenty-One

At the bottom of the stairs Charity let go of Rose's hand and dashed into the kitchen, calling, 'Mr Tompkins! Mr Tompkins!'

'Not seen him this morning, my dear,' Mrs Browne said, turning away from the stove. She lowered her voice to a whisper. 'No sign of your young friend, either. I hid him in the back scullery last night, poor boy, but he's not there now.'

Rose followed Charity into the kitchen. 'We are to have breakfast in the master's study today – come on.'

'I was just looking for Mr Tompkins.'

'I've already told you, he'll turn up, and Mrs Browne will spoil him as usual.'

Mr Delafield was at his desk, his back to the door. He was dressed in black, as if he were about to go to a funeral, with a high white collar and a black silk tie, held in place by a gold pin. He looked solemn.

'Good morning, sir,' Rose said, and made a little dip of her head.

'Good morning, Father,' Charity said, looking straight ahead, her eyes defiant.

'Good morning,' he replied. 'Well, not exactly a good morning, even though the sun is shining. A serious morning . . . a *difficult* morning might be a better description. Despite that, I hope it will mark the beginning of a new life for you, Charity. Please do sit.' He rang a little hand bell on the desk, and Edward came in. 'You may fetch the breakfast tray from Mrs Browne now,' Mr Delafield said over his shoulder.

Edward nodded his head and quickly winked at Rose and Charity before he left the room. Rose blushed a little.

'You seem very grave this morning, Rose,' Mr Delafield said.

Rose looked at the floor. 'I am sorry if I give that impression, sir. I cannot help but be troubled for my charge. It has come as a terrible shock to her to be sent away at once and so suddenly.'

Mr Delafield looked over at Charity, who sat very still, as if she had not heard a single word of their conversation.

'My daughter chose to disobey me and ran off with an uneducated youth to seek the undesirable company of a hysterical old woman. Sadly, I have been left with no alternative.'

Edward came back carrying a tray laid with a cooked breakfast for each of them. After he had put the tray down, he stepped back and stood to attention by the door.

'You may go,' Mr Delafield said with a

dismissive flick of his hand. He did not look round at Edward, who opened and shut the door but stayed just where he was.

'Eat well, my child. The carriage has been ordered shortly, and it will deliver us to the railway station. We have a long day ahead of us and you will need your strength.'

'I cannot, Father,' Charity said.

'Cannot,' her father said, 'or will not?'

'Both,' she told him.

'Now, now, Miss Charity – where are your manners this morning?' Rose said, leaning across to cut up the bacon on Charity's plate as if she were three years old again.

A plume of grey ash and soot fell down the chimney and billowed out onto the hearthrug, followed by a cloud of choking dust.

Mr Delafield stood up. 'What the blazes . . . ? I thought I'd paid Kawkins to clean the chimneys?'

After that everything happened in a fast and

frantic muddle, but to Charity it all seemed to be strangely slowed down. First a pair of skinny legs appeared above the mound of ash and soot in the fireplace. Then the rest of Silas tumbled down, and he climbed out of the grate.

'I found it,' he said to Charity with a grin. 'The room.'

Charity leaped up out of her seat. Rose tried to hold onto her sleeve, but the girl quickly pulled her dress free. Her father threw himself across his desk, scattering the breakfast tray and plates high into the air. She watched the plates smash and the eggs and rashers of bacon mingle with the smuts and ash. 'What do you think you are doing?' he shouted. 'How dare you!'

Charity was too quick for him. She dodged to one side, and joined Silas by the fireplace while her father tripped over the mess on the floor. Edward moved forward and helped him up. He continued to hold him tightly. 'There now, sir, calm yourself,' he said.

'Calm myself? What do you mean? Let go of me at once, you bumpkin!'

Edward tightened his grip, pinning his master against the edge of the desk. 'You two,' he said to Charity and Silas, 'run. Go and do whatever it is you have to do.'

'Are you mad too?' Mr Delafield cried, struggling to break free of Edward's grip.

'Ned, what *has* got into you?' Rose gasped.

'Nothing at all, as you well know.' Edward gave a broad grin. 'You called me Ned,' he noticed.

'You are both sacked with immediate effect!' Mr Delafield shouted, struggling in Edward's arms.

'Thank you, Edward,' Charity said. She took Silas's hand and pulled him after her into the hallway, slamming the door behind them.

Mrs Browne was bustling up the stairs. 'Whatever is happening in there? I heard shouting,' she said.

'Lock that door, Mrs Browne,' Charity called out.

'Bless you, m'dear – I don't have a key. Where are you off to?' Mrs Browne asked.

'To find my mother,' Charity said.

Mrs Browne looked astonished. 'Oh, my . . .' she murmured, then added quickly, 'I've never told you this before, as I had no wish to upset you, but I'm the only one here who really remembers your mother. A lovely, magical lady she was too. I loved her dearly. "Get the kettle on, Mrs Browne," she would say to me . . . I never believed she was dead, not for one minute. How I would love to see her smiling face again. You find her, miss – go on.'

Silas went over to the tall fireplace in the hall. 'This way,' he said, and pulled himself up inside it.

Mrs Browne watched, mouth open, as he pulled Charity up into the dark after him.

Chapter Twenty-Two

'So I was right about the hidden room?' Charity asked as they crawled along the narrow dark space.

'You were,' Silas said. 'I'm not sure I want to go in there again, though.'

Music drifted faintly towards them. It was the waltz that they had heard before. It swirled and drifted, and grew louder as they moved along. Charity had a picture in her mind of a ballroom, and of people in fine clothes, dancing. There was something odd about the tune, though. It was either off key or played wrongly; Charity would not have been able to explain it, but however pretty the music was, it also sounded sinister.

They reached the point where the narrow flue met the shaft leading to a chimney. There was a wide drop, straight down below them. The odd silvery light that Charity had seen flickering around the window was sparkling below them. The music was much louder now.

'I'll wait here,' Silas said. 'If you get into any trouble, I'll come and help.'

'Will there be trouble?' Charity said, and she felt a surge of energy again – the same feeling she had experienced in the forest. Smells and sounds drifted up and around her; the smells of animals and leaves and water.

'I'm going,' she said.

'I'll be here,' Silas told her. 'Don't forget.'

'I won't,' she promised, and lowered herself down towards the patch of light.

At first Charity couldn't understand what kind of

a place she'd come to. It was night, with bright moonlight filtering down from the ceiling – or was it the sky? The music was coming from the far end of the room, and there were shadowy figures dancing. All around her stood tall trees, and Chinese lanterns hung from the branches, trailing away into the distance.

Charity stepped out of the fireplace and walked further into the room. The dancing figures seemed to vanish and then reappear, in perfect time to the music. On the floor, between the trees, there was a carpet and a row of spindly chairs, shining gold in the moonlight. When she looked straight at them, there seemed to be people sitting in them, but she could see the chairs through them. *Ghosts*, she thought, and she understood why Silas didn't want to come back in if he didn't have to.

She could just make out a door which would lead out to the green corridor. Above it, hanging from a rope which disappeared up into the darkness beyond the ceiling, was a huge iron ploughshare. Just like the iron scissors over her old crib, Charity thought.

It was warm in the room – like a summer night. She moved forward, daring herself to walk past the dancing couples. If she had put her hand out to touch them, she was sure it would have passed straight through. As she walked into the room, the smells of the forest grew stronger, until she was deep among the dark trees. The canopy of leaves was so dense that even the bright moonlight hardly penetrated as far as the forest floor. When Charity looked down, the carpet had been replaced by a mass of twisted roots and plants. Everything seemed to be alive.

Alongside her, amidst the dappled pools of light, she noticed a black shadowy form. She stopped, and the shadow stopped too. She leaned forward and looked at it closely. A pair of green eyes stared back at her. It was Mr Tompkins.

'Oh, you bad cat!' Charity cried. 'I was so

worried about you.' She picked him up, and when she hugged him, she felt the comfortable engine of his purring. 'I thought I had lost you,' she murmured.

Beneath her feet, the thick tree roots were moving around like old, gnarled fingers. They even rose into the air as if to snake around her ankles and trip her up. Perhaps they would trap her here for ever. She quickly put Mr Tompkins down and they hurried on.

They had gone a long way into the trees when she saw a clearing lit by sparkling shafts of moon-light. In the middle stood a smaller tree with drooping branches – a weeping willow. On the ground beneath the tree there was a white shape – and beside it sat a figure: a woman.

Mr Tompkins bounded through the grass and nosed his way under the tree. Charity followed him, cautious now. She wondered if she should call out for Silas. There was something both attractive and terrifying about the shapes under the tree. She suddenly found that she could not move another step; she was trembling all over, even though it was a balmy summer night inside the room.

'I might be dreaming,' she said quietly to herself. 'How do you tell if you are dreaming?' She pinched herself hard on the arm and it hurt. She wasn't dreaming.

Scents drifted over to her from under the tree. One of them was strong, like the sweat of a warm horse. The other was fresh and sweet and familiar, like the trellis in the walled garden when it was covered in honeysuckle; like the smell when she had first opened her mother's diary.

The woman under the tree suddenly spoke. 'Where have you come from?'

Charity heard Mr Tompkins meowing. The woman spoke again. 'If I didn't know any better, I'd say that you were—'

'It's Mr Tompkins,' Charity said nervously, approaching the willow tree. 'I followed him here. He's my cat.'

The woman stood up and brushed down the skirt of her long green dress. 'I could have sworn he was my kitten,' she said. 'That's what he would have looked like fully grown. Come a little closer – let me see you.'

Charity stayed still for a moment, unable to move. Somehow she knew that voice. She stood there, staring at the woman.

'Well, if you won't come to me,' the woman said, stepping out through the curtain of willow branches, 'I'll come to you.'

The woman and the girl stood looking at one another, both lit by silver shafts of moonlight. Neither spoke. Mr Tompkins rubbed himself around Charity's legs, looked up at her and meowed.

Charity swallowed, unable to take her eyes off the woman's face. 'He's hungry,' she said. 'He missed his breakfast this morning. I was worried – I thought I had lost him.'

'Lost him?'

'Yes.' Charity was hardly able to speak; her throat felt dry and tight. 'Lost him . . . for ever.'

'It's hard when you lose things,' the woman said.

Charity was trembling more than ever now. 'There are ghosts dancing in this room,' she said.

'Not ghosts,' the woman told her. 'They are memories of my wedding party. My memories drift about here like moths. Were you scared by them?'

Charity shook her head. 'Not really. I think my friend was, though.'

'Your friend?'

'My friend Silas. He's a sweep's boy. He cleans chimneys all day long, poor thing.'

They both fell silent again. Charity could feel tears welling up and rolling down her cheeks. She suddenly started sobbing, and her body heaved with the force of it.

At once she was enfolded in a pair of arms, and held, almost crushed, in a tight embrace;

her whole being was flooded with warmth – and that wonderful sweet honeysuckle smell.

'I can feel your heart beating,' Charity said through her tears.

'I can feel yours too. It *is* you, isn't it? My dearest darling? My baby girl? My Charity?'

'Yes,' Charity sobbed, hugging her mother with all her strength.

They stayed locked tightly together while the warm summer air drifted around them and the music faded in and out.

Charity had no idea how long they remained like that. She opened her eyes, and she and Ariella looked hard at each other, as if drinking in every detail.

'You are my child, all right,' her mother said. 'Just look at your hair.'

'It needs lots of brushing,' Charity said. 'Rose does it seventy-five times in the morning and seventy-five times at night. Father says—' She suddenly fell silent.

'Father says what?'

'Father says that this is all nonsense. All this . . . He says I am mad, and I am to be taken away to a special rational school – now, this morning, this minute.' She began to cry again, her head resting on her mother's shoulder.

'Nothing like that is going to happen,' Ariella told her.

There was a noise behind them, and the white creature lying under the tree shook itself, tossing its head and its silvery white mane. It gave a sad sort of whinnying cry. Ariella took Charity by the hand. 'Come with me – quietly now,' she said.

They went over to the tree, and Charity saw that the creature lying there was a beautiful white horse with a forest-green ribbon round its neck. Its nostrils flared at the sight of her, and it got nervously to its feet.

Ariella patted the creature. 'Here,' she said. 'Feel.' She took Charity's hand and placed it on the creature's mane. Charity had never felt anything so soft; it rippled and shone silver in the moonlight.

'Silver and gold,' Ariella said. 'Your hair next to the unicorn's mane.'

'I knew it was a unicorn,' Charity whispered. 'I knew it.'

Ariella stroked the creature's flank. 'See? It is trembling, nervous. There are so few of its kind left. Your poor father injured this one when he was hunting.'

'I know,' Charity said. 'I found the book of stories – and your diary.'

Ariella smiled at her daughter. 'I knew you'd find them eventually. In that case, you know that in his folly and innocence your father actually tried to shoot this beautiful creature. To him, it was simply an amazing prize, the trophy of trophies – as if he hadn't enough of the poor hunted things in those cases all over the house.

'When your father fired a shot at this unicorn, its horn – its precious, magical horn – was blown clean off. It ran away and hid. I was injured too, but not badly, and I explained to your father what he had done, for it is a terrible crime to injure a unicorn. He was so sorry, and he was so young and handsome, and I fell in love with him, and he fell in love with me – it was that simple. I promised him that I would never tell a soul about what he had done to the unicorn, for I knew that if my people found out, he would be made to suffer.

'My people are the ancient folk, you see. I am one of the ancients, and ancients do not marry mortals. My family were so unhappy when I told them that I was to wed your father, and they tried to stop us, but they could see how much I loved him. Eventually they agreed.

'Our wedding day was as you saw it in my memories, scattered in this room. There was dancing and music and moonlight and fireworks. We were very happy. And then, a little later, I found I was to have a baby, my own sweet baby, and I was even happier. You see, my darling, you are like this beautiful gentle unicorn – a half faerie, a rare being in the mortal world. You were born at midsummer, and I was so happy, for that is such a propitious date.

'Then, when you were just a few months old, news came of the unicorn. It had finally returned to the ancients' village, and my people had discovered how it lost its horn; how it had been disfigured by my mortal husband's bullet. The ancients had held a trial, and had reached their verdict. They marched up to the hall, and demanded the life of your father and you, my child, in payment for the crime.

'I begged with them to spare you both. I told them that I would pay for the crime myself; I would abandon you, leave the mortal world, and retreat into a room in Stone Green Hall – the room where my wedding took place; a place where the mortal and magical worlds had once met. I would remain there, and care for the unicorn, alone. The ancients agreed, but they demanded your life too. I bargained, and they agreed that they would take you at the age of thirteen – unless the crime could be atoned for before then.'

'I'm almost thirteen,' Charity whispered.

Ariella smiled sadly. 'I know.' She stroked her daughter's hair and continued.

'First I was allowed to say goodbye to you both. When your father learned that he was to lose his wife and, eventually, his daughter, because of his own stupidity, he went mad with grief. He lashed out at your little toy unicorn, breaking off its horn.'

'The horn!' Charity exclaimed.

Ariella nodded. 'Kind Mrs Browne found it later that day. She thought it was simply an ornament, and it has been sitting in the scullery ever since – the key to this whole thing, as you will see.

'Once I was inside this room, the ancients cast

a spell to seal up the door, so that it could no longer be seen from the corridor. It was as if they were burying me, along with the truth about what Charles had done. They hung the iron ploughshare above the door, so that I could not tamper with the spell; iron repels magic, you see. That is how I disappeared, and how this became a lost room, a place that never existed. But although they sealed the door, they forgot to seal up the chimney . . . Once I realized that, I knew there was still a way to communicate with the rest of the house – and with you, for I had come to understand how the crime could be atoned for – by reuniting this poor beast with a horn.'

Charity's mind began to whirr. *The horn* . . .

'I couldn't communicate with my husband; he had no magic himself, and losing me had made him loathe and fear anything magical. He was distraught, and could no longer admit to himself what I was, and he had all traces of me removed to the west wing and locked away. He was terrified of losing you too, and he had a pair of iron scissors hung over your crib for protection, because he knew that one day the faerie would come for you.'

'That's why he's sending me away to school . . .' Charity said slowly. 'I'll turn thirteen this year.'

'And yet it would make no difference,' Ariella told her. 'They would find you there, just the same. Unless the crime can be atoned for before that day.'

'And you know how? It's all about the horn, isn't it?'

'Yes.' Ariella nodded. 'And as I knew I couldn't communicate with your father, I tried to contact you. I have been calling to you all this time – sending you the dream to lead you to the book, and the diary, and finally to this place. I sent a message to Sarah, and asked her to contact you once you were old enough to understand, and tell you to find the horn.'

'And I found it,' Charity said.

'Yes,' Ariella said. 'And now, you see, there is a way to save you – save us all, and put everything right.'

'But—' Charity didn't finish what she was about to say. There was a deafening banging and hammering, a sound like thunder, as if someone was attacking the walls. The unicorn reared up on its hind legs in terror.

'Silas!' Charity cried out, almost without thinking, and her friend dropped down from where he'd been waiting in the chimney.

'Where are you, Charity?' he shouted as another series of bangs shook the room.

'Over here,' Charity said, relieved to see his friendly soot-stained face appear through the trees.

When he saw Ariella and the unicorn, he paused nervously. 'It's true, then . . . Your mother was in here all along.'

'Yes,' Charity said.

There was another thunderous bang.

Ariella said, 'You must be my daughter's friend, Silas?'

He nodded.

'Could you help me hold onto this poor beast?'

The loud noises had frightened the unicorn and it was bucking wildly, trying to run away. Silas went over and put his sooty black hands on its silvery-white neck.

He looked into its eyes, and it immediately calmed down, lowering its head and standing there quietly. Silas reached up and stroked its mane. He whispered to the animal and it stopped trembling.

'It likes you, Silas,' Ariella said. 'It's a wonderful thing to see.'

'I like horses,' he explained. 'Always have. And they like me.'

There was another loud bang, and although the unicorn's eyes widened, it stayed still.

'It's not a horse, Silas,' Charity said.

'Look at its poor forehead,' Ariella added.

Silas studied the round, flat stump of horn.

'It is a very rare and special beast,' she told him.

There was another bang. 'I think we must be prepared for something,' Ariella said.

Suddenly a shaft of bright light penetrated through the trees. The wall had been breached, and they could hear voices.

Chapter Twenty-Three

'It's Father,' Charity said to Ariella.

'I knew it would be,' she replied. She closed her eyes and the music stopped playing; the ghostly dancing couples disappeared. The unicorn settled down under the willow, and Silas sat next to it, whispering softly into its ear and stroking its neck.

Charity saw her father and Sergeant Major Chambers coming towards them. Edward and Rose were walking a little way behind them, holding hands and looking around in disbelief at the strange scene – now a mixture of moonlit garden and sunlit furnished room. Sergeant Major Chambers was dragging a sledgehammer behind him. Charity could see where they had broken through the wall. The iron ploughshare was now hanging crookedly above the space where the door had once been.

Mr Delafield stopped in his tracks when he saw them both standing together in the bright patch of moonlight. Charity took her mother's slender hand and felt its grip tighten in answer to hers. Mr Tompkins trotted over to Mr Delafield, and he bent down and picked the cat up and stroked its head.

'I seem to have found your cat, Charity,' he said quietly, letting Mr Tompkins jump down again. He looked over at his beautiful wife, holding their daughter by the hand, and something inside him seemed to snap, as if a tight rubber band had suddenly been released.

'I never thought I would see you again, Ariella,' he cried out. 'Is it really you? Can it be?'

He began opening and closing his fists, and after a moment's hesitation he stumbled towards Ariella and Charity, flinging his arms wide while tears spilled down his face. Charity stepped back as her father and mother embraced. The wind blew through the leaves in a sudden squall and she caught the honeysuckle scent again. At first she thought that they were angry – so fiercely did they hold one another, they might almost have been fighting. Both had tears streaming down their faces, and Charity realized then that they were tears of happiness.

They stayed locked together for a long time. Then they kissed very tenderly, and Charity's father held her mother's face in his hands and looked into her eyes.

'I fell in love with your mother, Charity, the moment I looked into these eyes,' he said.

'It was the same for me, Charles – even though you could be so foolish,' added Ariella.

'You know I have not hunted since that day,'

he said. 'Oh, it is so good to hold you, my darling. Let us hold our daughter too.'

Charity fell into both sets of arms and was held and swung round and lifted up and down as if she were a five-year-old.

'She is so like you,' Mr Delafield said.

'I see you in her too,' Ariella murmured.

Rose, who had been watching everything, said to Edward, 'Tell me that we are dreaming this.'

'Oh, I am sure we are,' Edward said. 'While I think of it – have you made up your mind, Rose?'

'I have,' she said, and squeezed his hand.

Charity pulled free of her parents' embrace and turned to her father. 'We can help the unicorn,' she told him.

'How is that, my dearest darling girl?' he asked.

Charity reached into her pinafore pocket and pulled out the little twisted horn of carved wood. 'Here,' she said.

He stared at it, realizing what it was. 'Where did you get this?'

'I saw it on a shelf in the scullery with some old ornaments belonging to Mrs Browne. I don't know why, but I took it. Sarah told me to find the horn, but I had no idea that this might be it.'

'Your toy unicorn was cut and carved from the sacred yew grove,' Ariella told Charity. 'It is very special, and Mrs Browne has no idea what a wonderful thing she did by saving the horn.'

Charity handed the horn to Mr Delafield. 'You must do this,' she said.

'How do you mean?'

Ariella leaned over and whispered in her husband's ear. He took the little carved spiral and approached the delicate white creature, which began to back away at once.

'Whoa,' Silas said gently. The unicorn settled at once and stood with its head bowed. Mr Delafield, holding the horn out in his palm, seemed even more nervous than the unicorn. It tossed its head and gave a gentle whinny.

'Go on,' Ariella said. 'Just lift it into place. Heal the wound you made.'

Mr Delafield held the piece of wood against the stump of natural horn. A sudden gust of wind stirred the willow branches again, and a dazzle of silver sparkled under his hand like moonlight.

When he took it away, the horn remained in place. The unicorn reared up into the air, and its mane blew out in the wind. Silas spoke quietly to it.

'You have restored it,' Ariella told her husband. 'You have atoned for what you did. It had to be you, and no one else.'

'I was so foolish,' Mr Delafield said quietly. 'And I was cruel to you, Charity, when I did not mean to be. I was so frightened for you, my dear daughter. I was terrified of the threat that the ancients made, and my fear grew worse and worse as your thirteenth birthday approached, so that I was driven quite mad with it. I was sending you away to the school so that they would never find you' – he shook his head sadly – 'even though, deep down, I knew that they would find you wherever you were, and that there could be no hiding place from them.' He turned to his wife. 'What happens now?'

'What happens now is that I can finally leave this place,' Ariella said, 'and all the memories that have been my only company. We have nothing to fear from the ancients any more. The unicorn is restored.' She turned and looked at the noble silver-white creature, standing proudly in the moonlight. 'I can return to my life with you . . . that is, if you both want me.'

Mr Delafield's face suddenly looked as young as Charity could ever remember seeing it, as if the years had suddenly been lifted from him. Ariella smiled the oddly wild smile that had been captured in her portrait. Charity flung her arms around her mother again, but this time said nothing. There was no need for words.

'How do I explain all this to them?' Mr Delafield said, indicating Rose and Edward and the sergeant major.

'There will be no need. All this will seem like a very odd dream to them. They will barely remember that I was ever gone,' Ariella said.

'And I won't be going to the school now, will I, Father?' Charity asked.

'No, you won't,' he assured her. 'My first job, when I leave this enchanted place, will be to have the carriage dismissed.' He pulled Charity close to him, kissed the top of her head and smiled. 'Your hair looks very nice – just like your mother's.'

Silas spoke up. 'What will happen to this animal?'

'It will be free now,' Ariella said, 'as it should be. But of course, a rare and beautiful creature such as this is always at risk from those who would hunt it down. For mortals, this beast is a myth, a legend. It is no wonder that when they discover one, they want to possess it.'

'I don't like to think of anything bad happening to it,' Silas said. 'I could stay with it and protect it. It's not much of a life for me, going up and down those dirty chimneys all day – not compared to looking after this beautiful animal. And I would be in the open air.' He gestured around at the forest within the magical room. 'Does this all go on far beyond here?' he said, pointing to one of the paths leading away through the trees.

'This place goes on for ever,' Ariella said. 'I think you would be very happy here. I can see that you were meant to do this. Just look how the unicorn has responded to you.'

'But Silas,' Charity said, 'you are my first and only friend. You were the one who helped me to find my mother. If you leave, how will I ever see you again?'

'Simple,' Ariella said. 'You just have to agree to play hide-and-seek now and then, and make this room your hiding place.'

'Really?' Charity said.

'Really.'

Silas moved a little way along the path, and the unicorn turned to follow him.

'You see? It understands you, deep down, and that is the rarest of things – as rare as the beast itself,' Ariella said.

Silas shook hands with Mr Delafield, then bowed a little awkwardly to Ariella; finally he turned to Charity.

'You were very kind and brave to come with me,' she said, and extended her hands. Silas took them in his, and Charity noticed that there was no trace of soot on them any more. 'You're all clean now,' she told him.

'So I am. I'm saying goodbye to all the soot. I'll be here if you ever need me again.'

'I know,' Charity said.

Silas braced himself and then climbed up onto the unicorn's back. The creature did not move a muscle except to flick its tail.

'Goodbye, then, Charity . . . everybody,' he said. 'I will see you all again very soon, I hope.'

'You'd better.' Charity picked up Mr Tompkins and held him close. She thought she might cry.

Silas waved to them all and rode slowly away down the path. He was soon lost to view.

'What will we say to Mr Kawkins?' Charity asked.

'Oh, boys of his age run away all the time,' Mr Delafield said. 'We'll say he ran off to join the circus.'

'An equestrian act, of course,' Ariella added.

Mr Delafield took the sledgehammer back from Sergeant Major Chambers and ushered him, Rose and Edward back out into the corridor. Once through the smashed and broken wall, they all yawned and stretched, as if they had just woken up. Neither Rose nor Edward seemed in the least surprised to see Ariella.

'Edward,' Mr Delafield said, 'we will need to find a builder. Some work needs doing to this wall – see to it, will you?'

'Certainly, sir,' Edward said.

'Welcome home, Mrs Delafield,' Rose said with a polite little curtsey. 'It's very nice to meet you at last. I know that Charity has been so looking forward to you coming back.'

'Thank you, Rose,' Ariella said. 'I am very glad to be back after all this time.' She looked up and down the gloomy corridor – at the glass cases and hunting trophies. 'I intend to make some changes in this house,' she said. 'Everything looks very different to when I saw it last. We could do without all these dustsheets over everything, and I think we might get rid of all of these poor stuffed animals, don't you, Rose?'

'Yes, I do,' Rose said, smiling.

Ariella touched her husband on the arm. 'And

we no longer need those sharp iron railings – or those ugly great gates. We have nothing to fear from the ancients any more. We can live close to nature now – the forest need not be a place to fear. We can blow off all the dust and cobwebs at last. And summer will be on the way soon – we can start preparing for Charity's birthday party.'

As they walked along the green corridor, the leaf pattern on the wallpaper suddenly looked fresher and brighter. It was almost as if the old house knew that winter was finally at an end.

When they reached the kitchen door, Ariella called out cheerily, 'Now then, Mrs Browne, where's that kettle?'

Chapter Twenty-Four

It was morning. Charity woke and sighed to herself. She stretched and felt something move against her feet.

'Hello, Mr Tompkins,' she said, leaning forward and ruffling the cat's ears. He rubbed against her and purred. 'If Rose finds you in here, she'll put you out, and I'll be in trouble again.'

She lifted the cat down onto the floor. 'Shoo,' she said, and clapped her hands lightly, but Mr Tompkins just looked up at her with his mysterious green eyes.

'In a minute, then,' she told him. She knew that

at any moment, as regular as clockwork, Rose would come in and light the fire, as she did every morning, and another day would start, just like all the others.

Just like all the others . . . ?

It felt as if something was different. Had something happened? Charity wondered.

She had been dreaming again. A shadow passed over her – a sudden shiver of dread. It had been a dream, after all.

There was a click as the door opened. It was time to have her hair brushed.

'Morning, Rose,' she said, yawning again.

The curtains were quickly drawn, and bright sunlight streamed into the room.

'Wake up, sleepyhead, it's a lovely morning.'

A figure was silhouetted against the dazzle of sunlight from the bedroom window. It wasn't Rose. This person had a cascade of golden hair, which fell down over her shoulders.

'How are you this fine morning, my darling child?' Ariella asked. 'Come on – time to brush your hair.'

Charity's hair was fine and easily tangled, and depending on the light, sometimes it was the colour of bright gold, and sometimes it was the colour of flames.

'Hold still now,' Ariella said.

It used to hurt, whether she held still, or wriggled, and writhed, and screamed, and kicked her feet against the skirting board under the dressing table, as she once used to.

Charity smiled at herself and at her mother in the silver-edged glass.

It used to hurt.

Charity's hair was curly and knotted, and the brush was drawn in swift, gentle, easy strokes down her head with a static crackle.

'Mmm!' murmured the girl, who would not need to cry now – would never need to cry again.

'There – all done and no fuss,' said Ariella, who had been counting as she brushed. 'Seventy-five strokes, morning and night. Isn't that the rule?'

From the *County Mercury*
June 16th 1904

COUNTY MERCURY

ENGAGEMENTS

The engagement is announced between Mr Edward 'Ned' Cooper and Miss Rose Constance Marwick, both in domestic employment at Stone Green Hall.